HOLD THE LINE

REALITY BLEED BOOK 7

J.Z. FOSTER

WINTER GATE PUBLISHING

*Dedicated to Sigourney Weaver because of this line from **Aliens:***

"Get away from her, you bitch!"

You changed my life.

PROLOGUE

Before

ALEXANDER EGOROV'S days were mostly filled with monotony and boredom. He'd moved to Moscow for work sometime back when the munitions factory in Kiev automated.

He'd lost his job to those damn machines.

There'd been unrest and even riots, but he was sure to get out before it got too bad.

"Just go to Moscow. There's always work there," his grandfather had told him.

Alexander had been in awe of Moscow when he arrived. He marveled at the towering buildings that buzzed with life, and the food lines were far shorter than in Kiev.

He'd applied for a worker pass right away and was granted one for the energy sector, which sounded glamorous. He'd seen large-scale rigs pumping oil before, and the massive electrical facilities were the lifeblood of the Soviet Union.

But he should have curbed his ambitions, as he had no technical skills or training. Alexander indeed worked in energy, but he was little more than what they called a *rat*.

"Scurry in there, rat. Something is clogging the ventilation." It was among the first orders he'd received from his new manager when he arrived at work, and those same orders filled his days every day.

Thin of frame and more flexible than most, Alexander was the ideal *rat*. That might have seemed foolish to some, but not to him. He understood he was an important part of the Communist Party, and he completed tasks few other men could.

It was his duty to the Motherland to make sure the ventilation at this particular energy facility stayed clear, and he could take pride in that.

But this often led him to thoughts of *what came next*. What was the next stage in life for a *rat*? Of course, if the government asked him to clear ventilation for the rest of his life, he would do it, but just as the munitions factory had automated, *surely* something would happen here?

But a year passed, then two, then a few more.

And he still cleared the ventilation.

He'd gotten good enough that they would ask him to train other *rats*.

The trick was to suck your elbows in toward your chest, so that your hands were just above your chin as you climbed into the ventilation. The new people never got that. They always stretched their arms to crawl like a baby, but doing that forced their shoulders wide and caused most to get stuck.

Alexander would laugh at the men who didn't listen to his instructions, as they ended up getting stuck.

Of course, they'd pull the man out, and it was often painful. The man would have bruises or sore arms for a week, and they'd all have a good laugh.

It had always been funny except for a few weeks back.

They hadn't been able to pull the man out.

The man had screamed and cursed, but it was hard to even hear what he was saying.

"He should have tucked his arms in like I told him," Alexander had said to anyone who would listen. *"He should have listened to me."*

The manager had been distraught when he realized they couldn't get the man out. It wasn't because the man was slowly dying as the ventilation heated up from the blockage, but because the overheating was going to disrupt the work.

If production numbers came down, there would be hell to pay.

There was a discussion among senior staffing on how to get him out, and their conclusion had come quickly enough.

"Amp the heating to fry the blockage, then drag it out.

Someone had said that, but Alexander hadn't heard who. It was as if he'd heard it in a dream. It wasn't real.

At some point that night, he'd plopped down in a seat and grew deaf to the screams and shuffling of the staff as they got *the blockage* out. If he'd been thankful for anything that night, it was that they didn't ask the *rat* to clear the blockage after they cooked it.

He had to wonder now, every time he opened a new shaft porting to crawl inside, what would happen if he got stuck?

But in reality, it wasn't a question at all.

He knew what would happen.

If production numbers came down, there would be hell to pay, after all.

It was strange now to finally *wake up* to how the world really worked. He'd had a strange sense of optimism before, but now he knew his real value to the Motherland.

But there were things more important than a rat, weren't there? He told himself that often. Perhaps, if he worked hard enough and never complained, he could receive a new position somewhere else and leave the *rat* life behind him.

Or maybe one day he'd get stuck and need to be cooked to a crisp so he could be more easily dragged out.

In his high-rise apartment, which smelled faintly of piss, he was sitting at his kitchen table eating reheated soup and considering that very thought when his television flipped on by itself.

There was a loud buzz and flash of light signaling an incoming message.

It wasn't an uncommon thing. The state had the power to turn TVs on so as to deliver a message, but it had startled him, as he hadn't expected it.

Alexander set the soup down and walked over to the TV. He expected a suit and tie reporter or perhaps some government official with reports on the grand schemes of their leaders, or warnings of terrorist activities.

But this time there was no man in a suit. Instead, the screen flashed to a person with a featureless CAG helmet, so polished Alexander could see the gleam from the cameras focusing on the helmet. The soldier stood in front of a black backdrop.

"All citizens are ordered to remain indoors." It was a man's voice, though hard and metallic from being processed through the internal speakers of the armor, giving it an inhuman quality. *"A contagion has been leaked, and terrorists are active. Governmental forces have moved in to subdue the threat. Do not open your door in any situation."* He paused long enough that Alexander thought the whole screen might have frozen. *"Those residing in the Eastern districts of Moscow are required to secure their doors. Do not open your door under any circumstance."* He insisted once more. *"Any citizen caught outside their residence will be shot."* He leaned in, and the lights shone off his helmet.

"Do not. Open. Your door."

The television clicked off.

Alexander stood dumbfounded. He'd never seen such a broadcast. What was he supposed to do?

That was easy enough.

Stay inside.

But terrorists inside Moscow? It must be something big. The government had squelched terrorists before, but never with such concern on television. In fact, usually the TV stayed on to broadcast the executions.

It was oddly silent now.

He went back to his table and quietly ate the rest of his soup.

Everything seemed fine enough, just like any other day. The only sounds in his room were the buzz of electricity and the hum of machines along with the clink of his spoon against the bowl.

He finished the soup and left it there. While crossing his arms over his chest, he wondered what was happening outside.

He glanced toward his outside wall. Though he lived on the eighteenth floor, he didn't have much of a view. He had to drag a chair over and stand on it to look out the small port window high in the wall.

Why the government had built his dwellings with no window or even with the small one so oddly placed, he had no idea, but he occasionally wondered about such things.

Standing on the chair, he had to lean up on the tips of his toes to get his nose just above the ledge to look out.

He couldn't see anything particularly strange or bothersome. His window did face the East, but he hardly had a clear view with so many buildings clogging his vantage point.

"Hmm," he grunted.

Whatever was happening, it wasn't worth losing sleep over. He climbed down and rolled his head around, stretching out his aching neck. He headed toward the bed. He had to press hard on a wall to make it click, and then his bed folded out from a compartment.

With a yawn, he pulled his jacket off and tossed it aside and prepared to sleep the rest of the night away.

ALEXANDER'S EYES jolted open as his room rattled, and the electricity flashed off. Seconds ticked by in utter silence.

Alexander did nothing. He only froze in place, his mind didn't bother to consider what had happened until things settled down.

Just like a rat.

The rattling stopped, and the electricity returned. The orange glow of a light set high in his room flashed, indicating some kind of emergency.

He tossed aside his blanket. His apartment had never rattled like that before.

"The hell was that...?"

The heating must have turned off, as he could see his breath as he spoke. He tugged his jacket back on and went over to the chair by the wall. He stretched up toward the window.

His heart nearly froze. The lights were completely off in the far eastern district, and several buildings laid in rubble.

"Oh my God. . ."

He rubbed the window with the end of his sleeve, but it was dirty on the outside and hard to see clearly. He squinted. Small flashes of light glowed in the distance.

Was it rifle fire?

He stretched on his toes to lean closer to the window when the TV popped on again, startling him so much he fell off the chair.

He smashed onto the floor and groaned, but there was no time to wait as he scurried toward the beep, which indicated an oncoming message.

An attractive blonde woman—Alexander recognized her as a reporter but forgot her name—was breathing hard and focusing on the screen, a building burned behind her.

"There has been another accident." She glanced at something off screen. *"A low-yield nuclear weapon has been ignited within Moscow."*

Alexander clinched his hands in front of his mouth and moaned. *"Oh my God,"*

The woman continued, "All citizens are being reminded to *lock-down*. Stay inside, lock your doors and—" A dark shadow barreled into the woman and the camera flashed around losing focus.

Alexander stayed so still that he didn't even breathe. People were screaming, but who or why, he didn't know.

The camera cut off and a black screen came on. Words in white flashed on it.

Lock your doors.

1

Now

"So, Rat, where are we going?" Miles asked as he followed behind the short Russian man.

"Just ahead, friend." Rat pointed with a half curled finger down an alleyway. "There's a safe place here."

Kevin whispered, "I feel like he's going to eat us."

Miles slapped Kevin with the back of his hand. "What's your plan here, *friend*? You found a place to hide?"

Rat grinned back at him and showed his missing teeth. "Just here." He moved up toward a door and wrapped his bony fingers around a large metal handle. He twitched as he looked either way and then slid the door open and scurried inside.

"Little bastard does move like a rat," Miles whispered toward Kevin.

"Like I said, I think he might try to *eat us.*" Kevin's eyes flared open.

Miles puffed out air. "I'll take my chances, mate. Better him than something else." He moved inside. Kevin followed behind him and then pushed the door closed.

"I can't see a damn thing in here." Miles glanced either way but the whole place was dark. "Where'd you go, Rat?"

"Here." He struck a match and lit a candle. He set it down on a table. "This is an old factory. We are safe here."

"Good to know." Kevin let out a breath and peeked back at the door.

Rat grinned above the candle light. "My English is good, yes? I watch so many American movies. You are Americans?"

"No, mate." Miles approached shaking his hand. "I'm English, and my pal here is Australian. Not a drop of American blood between us."

Rat's grin faded and his eyebrows curled up in disappointment.

Miles fought back his irritation, and instead grinned. "But you like movies? Ever see any TV shows or documentaries?"

Rat frowned.

"Come on." Miles nodded and pointed up at his face.

Rat's frown deepened.

"Maybe it's the light. You ever see *Westwood's Wild World?*"

"Westwood's what?" Rat answered.

Kevin scoffed. "He doesn't know who you are Miles, get over it."

"Piss off, I don't care if he recognizes me. I'm just surprised someone into Western media wouldn't know."

Kevin chopped both hands out in front of him and gestured first at Miles and then at the door. "There's fucking aliens out there eating people. What's it matter if he recognizes you or not?"

"So you are in movies?" Rat interrupted.

"Doesn't matter." Miles waved him off. "My hateful pal here has a point. What in God's good name is going on now?"

Rat hissed through his missing teeth and shook his head. "We had uhh. . ." he looked for the word. "TV show that told us there was a problem." He nodded content.

"Oh, yes, you have a fair bit of a problem here," Miles agreed. "But how did it happen?"

Rat shook his head. "I don't know."

Kevin exchanged a look with Miles. "Do you know which direction it came from?"

"It started. . ." Rat pinched his lip and pulled it as his eyes moved side to side. "*East*? This way is East?" He pointed.

"Aces, mate." Miles gave him a thumbs up. "So it started in the East and came this way?"

Rat bobbed his head. "Now most the monsters are gone."

"Most are gone?" Kevin twisted his head. "Where'd they go?"

Rat made a gesture with his fingers as if they were walking and then pointed west. "That way. Many are still here, but there were *so* many before. I saw them attacking and I stayed here until it was quiet. When I went back out, I found you. But there are still some in the city that are, uhh—" His eyebrows turned up again, and he put on a fake smile. "Hunting? But all we do now is wait here, yes?"

Miles scratched his chin. Maybe he was insane, but sitting here in the dark with a man called Rat didn't sound all that appealing when there was still a story out there. "They came from the East you said? Think I might take a look myself."

"Hey. . ." Kevin's voice flattened.

"I'll have myself a look, that's all." Miles glanced at Kevin. "You oughta stay here though, might be easier with just one pair of legs."

"No, no, no!" Rat swiveled his head back and forth, like it might just roll off. "There was uhh." He winced trying to find the word and frowned deep. He made a whistle and gestured his fist down then mocked an explosion. "*Big* bomb."

Miles huffed out a laugh. "Far more concerned about the aliens than the bombs, mate. I can deal with the wreckage. Debris doesn't try to bite your bits off." He grabbed his crotch.

"*No*." Rat closed his eyes and searched for the word. His eyes popped open. "Nuke. Atomic." He gestured his hands into a mushroom cloud. "Atomic bomb."

Kevin pointed his finger at Rat. "You telling me the lunatics are dropping nuclear bombs on Moscow?"

Rat glanced away, considering if he understood before nodding. "Yes." He didn't seem all that surprised. "The bomb is that way. You will be very sick."

Miles gestured his arms out. "So the plan then is to do nothing except sit here and cry in the dark and hope things end up not being tits up? Shit on that." Miles made a gesture like his fingers walking. "We can walk around the blast site."

Kevin puffed out air. "For a guy who did a show on weird shit, you don't seem to know a lot about radiation. The wind could blow it right into your face and then you're growing fingers out of your ass."

Miles winced. "You paint a truly horrifying verbal picture there, but no, I do know a *wee* little bit about nukes." Miles held his fingers an inch apart. "And I'm willing to bet my life on them using a tactical warhead that doesn't throw out radiation everywhere. The lunatics wouldn't want to make their capital irradiated for a thousand years. They just want a *nice* firestorm as hot as the sun to melt some aliens and when all's said and done, they'll roll the cleanup crews in and swab everything down. There will be a small irradiated zone, and we just avoid that hellish place."

Miles knew he had him then when Kevin looked away to consider if that was true. Rat on the other hand looked unsure of what was even being said.

But Miles? He was full of shit. He may not know much about nuclear weapons, but one thing he did know was how to *sound like* he knew anything. Everything else was theoretical. And he certainly wasn't going to sit on his ass when he could be out getting footage.

"Look." He held a hand up flat while he pulled his bag off. Being a few years out of practice didn't matter, Miles still knew how to put on a show. He set his bag down and dug things out and lined them up on the table. "Let's see here. Socks. Protein bars. Ahh, here we go." He pulled out a bottle of pills and shook it. "Rad pills. Keeps the junk out of your blood."

"You have *rad pills* in your damn bag?" Kevin spoke as if he didn't believe it.

"What can I say, I'm a boy scout, mate. Always be prepared. I've been up to my elbows in low radiation environments before. You pop a few of these little chicklets and you're as good as gold."

"Don't they turn your piss orange?"

"Red in my experience, but I always double dose. Figured if one's good, two's better. Doctors can shove that recommendation up their arse." Miles clicked his tongue off the end of his teeth and sighed. "So here's where I'm sitting. I already took an eye out for this little adventure—you still have that little bastard in your bag don't you? I plan on putting that back into my skull—so I'm not going to let a little thing like *radiation poisoning* slow me down. If I get into any trouble I'll just shove a few of these pills up my bum and be right as rain."

"You have to stick them up your arse?" Kevin frowned deeply.

"Here." Miles held out his hand. "Give me the camera and you hold down the fort with Rat here. I'll be back in no time and we'll get to—"

"You think I'm just going to sit here?" Kevin flung his hands up and then grabbed his bag. "I'm going with you. We're going to get those photos of where they're coming from and *then* we'll head back."

"It's getting hairy, Kevin. You sure you're still in? I mean, I'm still up to my knees in lawsuits from my ex-wife, but you didn't sign up for crawling through wreckage and getting eaten by an alien." Miles frowned. "When we agreed, I figured the worst might be that a commie might shoot you."

"I'm not interested in the money—I'm interested in the truth." He flashed his eyes at Miles. "Where the shadows are deepest, the secrets are darkest."

Miles barked out a laugh. "Did you just quote my show to me? *The secrets are darkest.*" Miles mocked the line he had said so many times before. "You know that was some goofy shit a writer came up with right? It doesn't make any sense. But, oh, I like the spirit." He slapped Kevin on the arm.

Kevin smiled enthusiastically.

Rat cleared his throat. "I will go too?" He grinned wide. "I am very interested."

"You kiddin'?" Miles pointed at Rat. "You're going to show us where the ugly bastards came from."

"That's it then." He waved toward the door. "Let's go get some pictures of some ugly ass aliens."

2

THERE WAS A TIME, before his ascendency, where Lei Zhao had lived as a peasant. He had once, long ago, walked the dirt streets of Beijing, and stared up at the mighty dark tower in the center of the city.

He looked up at it with envy and spite. He hadn't understood its real purpose.

It was the nail that held China together.

People are meant to be ruled.

It was a truth he now understood. And despite all the empty words thrown from Western governments, he knew the way of China, and he knew his people.

When the revolution had come to sweep away the old dynasty, he had been amongst the first to draw up a weapon.

He'd led the charge that stormed the tower, and he himself had kicked in the door to find the cowering leader who had feasted while his people starved.

Zhao had been so sickened by the crying man that he had let others take him away.

It had just so happened that Zhao was looking out the window of the marvelous palace when he saw the screaming man fall from the sky.

The coward had been thrown from the roof.

So high was the place that Zhao had not seen the man land, but strangely, as if the picture had been burned into his mind, Zhao remembered the man's screaming face as he fell.

That day, Zhao had become leader of a new China. One who did not bow to Western whores or hypocrites who had seized upon China like mad dogs when it was weak, and now criticized the way the Chinese people were ruled.

Zhao lived in the tower now, and he walked the same floors that the old government had. He understood now that this was not a place to be envied. There was work here, important work. He partook in the same luxuries as the last ruler. Such things were important because of the one truth in the world.

People are meant to be ruled.

The masses would not respect a man who ate the same food as them. They would not fear a man who walked the same dirt roads.

They wanted a man who looked down upon them with the same eye as a god.

A god would garner respect.

A man would not.

So long as the work was done.

That should not be forgotten, lest Zhao find himself flying from the roof of the tower.

So Zhao lived up high in the tower that nailed all of China together.

And he was not weak.

Some starved, yes, but China had grown strong. In a few short years, China had gone from a beggar's kingdom, to one of great international power.

All as the West watched on with envious eyes, just as Zhao had.

The West would preach to him of human rights while their companies took water from thirsty nations. The West would cry foul of his military ambitions to draw in rogue provinces all while the Western nations attacked foreign countries with impunity.

And the West wanted the same for China as they had for

themselves.

Women as whores, and men as liars.

Zhao only wanted his people not to starve.

And to be respected.

China had been powerful once.

It would be again.

Many would suffer to that end, but all Zhao had to do was remember that China had once been broken by its enemies, that it had once cowered and starved, and pleaded for food and medicine.

China would never beg again.

So Zhao would stand there in the tower and look down, and he would sip a fortune in drink as the people of China built upon his grand designs, not because he enjoyed it.

But because people are meant to be ruled.

And China would never beg again.

He was standing in the tower right now, looking out the exact same window where he had seen the premier falling, and he was watching the chaos outside.

Something had happened in one of their research facilities, he didn't know precisely what, but it was spreading a madness throughout the city.

The People's Army had assembled now and quarantined the blocks of the city, yet it still spilled out and was quarantined again.

He could see the fighting, even from here. He knew those streets, he had walked on them himself.

He'd been told they were some kind of demon, that this was perhaps the end of an age, but no.

He set his glass down and crossed his arms behind his back. He would watch for a time more before he got to work.

This was not the end of an age.

This was just the beginning.

———

THREE KINGS. Three crowns. Three to rule the world.

Three Archons were born and one had entered the world and waited for his brothers.

Their time had come.

Men had built a gate and he, the Archon, stepped through.

He'd come through as a pale and wet being, a new god born to the world.

His children came with him.

Mad with hunger and a thirst for blood, they frenzied upon the screaming scientists. As they ate and killed, knowledge flowed to the Archon.

Beijing. China. Jade.

With that, he took a name.

The Jade Archon.

The name flowed through the hive mind and his children stopped to scream his praise.

He walked the halls of the compound as chaos erupted around him. His children, fresh from the gate, darted around him, though all were careful not to brush him lest they incur his wrath.

They flowed onto the streets and men with weapons came to stop them, but this world was rife with meat, and each dead became a new soldier for the war.

Humans infected with parasites formed the bulk of the forces that flowed against the armies of the men. And each time their enemy formed a perimeter, the Jade Archon's children smashed it.

They would soon take this world and reshape it, and give all it had to the Mother.

But it was not for the Jade Archon alone.

He was but one of three.

Three kings. Three crowns. Three to rule the world.

Amidst the screams of dying men and the roaring of his children, the Jade Archon found a small patch of dirt and knelt down to it.

His mind and body were fresh. He did not know much of this world, but there was another who could show him.

He reached for his eldest brother, the first king.

The shadows of the hive mind were dark and its pathways were like syrup. A strange thickness made it difficult to connect with his brother, but the Jade Archon found him and reached for his brother's mind.

There were no words to describe such a place, as it had no form, but his brother's mind lived in a place darker than shadows, and deeper than night. It was thick with webs that made it hard to reach.

And it crawled with hate and pain.

But the Jade Archon reached inside for his brother, into the thick shadows and the painful void.

In the hive mind, there were no blades or sharp edges, but had there been, then his brother's mind was cut like a dagger's edge.

The Jade Archon pulled back painfully, his mind bleeding from the attempt.

A strange anger and madness flooded across him like a disease.

Something horrible had happened to his brother, and it had changed him.

His brother was insane.

Three kings? Three crowns? Three to rule the world?

No.

As the Jade Archon closed himself from the hive mind and stood up from the dirt, he realized.

This world would have to be different.

MOSCOW BURNED and The Archon felt a bubble of air moving toward the surface of his skull. It was sliding through his brain and it was making his eye twitch in a way he couldn't control.

Electrical shocks sizzled through his body as the air popped up on his skin.

Psst.

And he felt new tissue knit there to fill the gap.

He was annoyed.

Today should have been a day of triumph.

The Archon had broken *Moscow* and it had become the throne

upon which he would build the new world.

But he was not satisfied.

The woman.

He'd sent the Harbinger to collect her, and just as he knew the intentions and mind of his children, he had felt the woman and knew where she would be.

His Harbinger had arrived there first and waited.

But something was different.

The Archon was distant from that fight, and it required focus to feel another, but he had felt the woman's mind as it snapped the bonds of the Harbinger.

He'd felt her strain as she turned the Archon's children against the Harbinger.

The Archon was not angry with her, no, he only further enticed.

But annoyed that she was so distant.

"I want the woman," he said out loud with human words, and his small beastial children near him stirred in a frenzied praise from hearing his voice.

The small sulking brood had followed him back toward the bunker, where it had all begun. With no real understanding of his command, they turned on each other and began to rip pieces off their brothers to offer as tribute.

The Archon took no notice as he stepped through the snow. The radiation that seeped off him burned and blacked the area.

He looked down onto the bunker. His children dragged screaming uninfected humans inside to be put through the gate.

The humans howled and screeched as the hands of the cronux held them in place and took them inside.

The Archon watched for a moment before he headed inside one of the large cargo elevators.

Cronux had morphed and evolved for purposes necessary to expand the empire, and some were now suited for menial jobs. A large worm-like creature with pink skin folds sagged down over the elevator controls. Its large lips sucked over the buttons and small tendrils tapped the commands.

The Archon felt the elevator begin to shift and all at once his vision hazed and the strange drunken blur came onto him.

Three kings. Three crowns. Three to rule the world.

His brothers had come.

He felt one reaching for him, the Jade Archon.

The Jade Archon's touch was light, soft and clean.

The scarred Archon was not. His mind had become a place of disease.

As the Jade Archon reached, their minds touched, and the scarred Archon knew what his brother knew. He saw the ripe city of Beijing and the people screaming within.

A city larger than Moscow with more people to command

A greater faith to spread.

Three kings. Three crowns. Three to rule the world.

But a thought came to him, and not for the first time.

Why need there be three when one would suffice?

He shoved away his brother, and their minds wrenched painfully apart.

Scarred. Damaged. Mutilated.

Broken.

He heard those thoughts from his brother before they disconnected.

So it would be then. He would be the scarred Archon. Hadn't he broken Moscow alone? Hadn't he been savaged by the atomic fires of men but still lived?

Was he not still beautiful?

"One king," he said that out loud and the children screamed in praise and agreement, for they were his slaves, and his alone.

And what of the Mother? What would she think?

But again, why need the scarred Archon share the gift with his brothers when he could simply give it to her alone?

Those thoughts had come with a darkness that swirled and swallowed him.

He blacked out.

Endless darkness was all that he was aware of, and it was neither pleasant nor frightening.

It simply *was*.

He came to again and the elevator had stopped.

The worm that controlled the elevator was throbbing on the ground. Chunks had been torn from it and its internals had spilled out onto the floor. Its large flapping mouth gaped open and closed while the tendrils shook in all directions.

The Archon's hand was coated in its blood.

How or why he'd done it, he didn't know.

Nor was it much of a concern.

He left the dying thing within the elevator and moved into the halls of the bunker.

His children went mad and tore at the walls as he passed, his presence so enthralling that they could not contain their excitement.

One group was pulling a human toward the gate, but was overwhelmed and tore at the captive, spilling blood everywhere. The frenzy soon spread, and every human in the hallway was shredded.

The Archon passed them all, and the radiation poured from him. The strong had their skin blister, and the weak curled up and died as their bodies crisped.

The Archon entered into the gate room. It pulsed with green energy. Much like the worm in the elevator, other cronux had evolved for the controls of the room.

Slender and bony cronux leaned over commands with long finger-like appendages that hit buttons. They had no mouths, and would surely starve to death before long, but their replacements would take their place before that could happen.

This was the way of the cronux.

This was how they ate worlds.

The Archon moved to the gate and he felt the Mother's presence.

An inky darkness seemed to seep through the gate and into his mind. It was not here in the real world, but part of the hive mind.

The darkness spread around him, drowning out color and distraction. Her mind took his, and her presence had weight.

His mind was diseased and sharp. It cut his brother.

But hers? It burned.

He felt her mind press down on his and he collapsed to a knee, and his chin angled toward the ground. Her heat rippled through the folds of his mind. He dare not look upon her, even within the hive mind, lest her love shatter him.

It was his place to speak, for her words were rare and beautiful. They were not given easily.

"This world is ripe," it was said not in words but in feeling.

That was all that was needed. Her darkness pulled from him and he could take to his feet once more.

The lines of cronux continued to hammer humans through the gate, dumping them into the green beyond.

There, within the pulsing gate, were the shadows of the *Fathers*, taking the offerings with their long arms and pointed fingers.

The humans screeched in useless horror, and were one by one dumped inside.

The Archon was not here for their screams.

He was here to build an army.

Come. I have need of you.

He sent the message through the hive mind and he waited.

Moments later large dark shapes formed near the edge, for they had been waiting for his call.

One by one, the commanders of his army stepped inside.

Janissaries.

Each a loyal servant of her will.

Four in all.

The Archon was young by comparison. He was formed by the Mother's desires and crafted for this world, but the Janissaries were each ancient and old in the ways of conquest. Still, they bowed their heads in submission to his greater purpose.

Each would take a portion of the Archon's army and spread the faith across the world.

But the Archon himself had plans.

He would go toward the woman.

And he would break the world.

3

ROLES POURED himself a drink and lazed back in his seat as he prepared to watch the first speech of his new president, John Winters, from a TV inset on the wall of his office.

This'll be good.

Roles took a drink.

John approached the podium and looked characteristically stern. He stared into the screen and began, "*My fellow Americans.*"

Roles took another drink.

John kept talking, but the words weren't important to Roles. They rarely were. People said more with their bodies than they ever did with their mouths.

"*...through a time of great pain...*"

John's back was stiff, and his voice was steady, but it was his eyes that were speaking volumes.

"*...will stop at nothing to...*"

His eyes were tight and focused, but not in a way that seemed natural, no, this was manufactured. Roles could imagine John Winters staring into a mirror minutes before and practicing that look.

John had been a staple of the U.S. Senate, and often described with words like *Rogue Element* within his party. There had been many publicized moments where Senator Winters had given a thumbs down to his party's policies in order to side with the opposition to applause and cheers within the media.

Of course, the voice that sometimes shifts has more power than the one that can be counted on.

John knew politics. But all men get old.

All men die.

The few remaining pieces of President Warren were a testament to that.

Roles was certain John Winters had enjoyed every bit of the applause, and he was equally certain that John never met a television interview he didn't love.

John's face was practically guaranteed to be on the news every night, and if it wasn't before, it was going to be now.

Hope you enjoy it.

Roles took another drink.

"...justice will be..."

He turned the TV off. He'd heard all he needed to hear. His break was over.

Back to work.

He reached over from his desk and grabbed a file that was marked an old red stamp.

URGENT.

Roles himself had been the one to see a lot of critical communications moved away from emails and back to hard copies.

You can't hack a hard copy.

That was something he was fond of saying, though it wasn't one hundred percent true. He'd seen plenty of documents wind up in enemy hands before.

In fact, he'd stolen some himself.

Still, hard copies were best. It was all about risk reduction in the intelligence game.

He leaned back into his chair and opened the file.

It was on the sleeper cells and the host of assassinations that had been conducted. Nearly all the top levels of U.S. leadership had been decapitated in a single night.

Nearly.

Roles was still here after all. Still the chief of Intelligence and Operations coordinator.

He paused to take a drink before he read again.

The report wasn't a dry read as far as reports go, but nothing was particularly surprising, though the conclusion was interesting.

MOLE SUSPECTED WITHIN WHITE HOUSE.

Interesting, yes, but surprise? Not quite.

No one else would ever read the report.

Roles would make sure of it.

Clearing his throat, he closed the file back up and sat it down on his desk.

Then he took another drink.

AFTER THE ADDRESS at the Oval Office, as the cameras and staff rolled out, John Winters had to take a moment to himself.

Even that felt selfish.

Tick. Tick. Tick.

The countdown of the Doomsday clock was in his head.

But he needed time alone to think and breathe, if only for a few minutes.

John had taken a seat at the Resolute Desk in the Oval Office as he'd given his address, but as soon as the cameras were off, he got out of it.

It didn't feel right.

Somehow, he felt like he'd stolen it, as if all this happened because he desired it.

But he really hadn't.

There had been a time, when he was far younger, that he had ambitions of one day being president.

As he'd grown older, he came to understand what was required to take the office.

Compromise.

Not by way of negotiation or bipartisan agreement, but moral compromise.

To build a coalition to win the presidency, it required that a person be many things to many people.

John didn't want that.

He didn't want to compromise his morality.

They're going to tell you to drop the bomb, John.

That was the thought going through his head.

He was well aware of what came next.

How could you not after this?

One of the first things he'd been informed of upon assuming the presidency was that for whatever reason, the Soviets had not launched any of their missiles. But even now, thousands of Americans were in secure military facilities, carefully watching for any indication that Soviet missiles launched.

And for John, just out the door was a military aid who carried a suitcase with commands capable of launching all of America's missiles upon its enemies.

One call and he could destroy the world.

God help us.

John crossed his arms and looked at the desk.

He didn't sit in it.

They're going to tell you to drop the bomb, John.

The thought ran through his head again.

How could you not after this?

———

JOHN DIDN'T HAVE a choice in the Situation Room. He'd taken the seat at the head of the table that was now lined with generals and officials.

He'd been right on what to expect.

They wanted Armageddon.

"We need to launch our missiles at their sites right now and seize the initiative," one general said, and John simply listened.

Another pointed out that if there was ever a time to end the war, it was now. "The Soviet Union is on its heels. We have to take control of the war before it gets further out of hand."

John only listened.

And it kept going.

"...move ground forces in and seize forward positions..."

And going.

"...that's all those bastards understand..."

And going.

"...no other option..."

For them it wasn't a question of dropping the bomb or not, but simply *how many* nukes were required to finish the job.

John listened until he'd had enough.

"I'll think about it," he said when the last military official spoke.

They scoffed and some tried to convince him.

He turned his eyes on them and gave as flat a look at possible.

"I'll think about it."

He dismissed them and they all gathered their things and left.

They thought he was weak, that he wasn't the right man for action.

Maybe they were right.

"Roles," he said just as the man was about to leave the room. "Come here."

John stood up from his seat and waited for Roles to approach. For whatever reason, he always preferred to be eye level with the man.

Roles stepped over quietly and stood with his back straight and his hands clasped in front of him. "Sir," he said respectfully but his eyes seemed bored.

"Where's my daughter?" John asked flatly.

"Sir," Roles repeated again and then took several irritatingly long seconds to reply. "She was in a recovery mission and last I was aware, she touched down in West Germany. I don't keep the particulars on any one mission so I—"

"Like hell you don't." John had to keep his voice from rising.

"You find out where she's at and inform me by tomorrow. Then you figure out how to get her back here. The situation's changed now."

"Sir," Roles said once more, and at this point John was certain he was doing it sarcastically. "Your daughter agreed to join the mission. She wasn't ordered into place."

"And now her father is president of the United States. If the Soviets get a hold of her, there's no telling what they'll do. Get her back here, Roles."

"Yes, sir." Roles nodded, his face never changing at any point.

John dismissed him and waited for Roles to step out of the room before he mumbled.

"Prick."

JOHN HAD KEPT the surviving members of Warren's team in place, and McAndrews became his Chief of Staff, setting the agenda.

John felt like little more than a hood ornament as things continued on the way as President Warren had planned them. John sat in on meetings, but more as an observer than anything else as members discussed economic policy and war structuring. He'd come to the White House so recently that he hadn't had time to even learn who everyone was.

But a change in leadership or not, the world kept turning.

"The issue is that the unions won't agree with the new policy changes," one man was saying.

"It doesn't matter, they made promises when we agreed to the terms of their pensions," a woman replied.

John cleared his throat. "What are the policy changes and what are the terms of their pensions?"

The room went silent and everyone turned to him. The man, and John didn't even know his name, spent the next twenty minutes trying to explain the coordination with the district's union inside the highway restructuring plan.

John nodded along like he understood, but in fact, he'd actually forgotten what the topic of the meeting was about.

He kept quiet the rest of the time.

At the end of the day, he dismissed everyone and went back to the Oval office to privately review documents on all current policies. It was an hour or more into the night before his secretary buzzed in to tell him that former president Jude Scott wanted to place a call.

Scott had lost his bid for a second term to Warren.

John wasn't sure why the man was calling, but decided to go ahead and take it.

It began as expected, with Scott telling him he was sorry for the circumstances, and that if there was anything he could do to help, he would, and John thanked him for that.

But then his voice turned cold.

"Mr. President, there's a man you need to talk to. Normally each outgoing president introduces him to the incoming president, but that wasn't possible this time, so he contacted me to make the introductions."

"What are you talking about? This some sort of lobbyist?"

"No, nothing like that."

"Then what is it?"

"He's got the book, Mr. President. The Book of Secrets."

John had heard of *The Book.* Supposedly it was written by presidents, for presidents. A history of America's secrets, too dangerous for all but a select few in Washington.

John rubbed his eyes. He was tired, and all he really wanted to do now was go to bed. "Is this real?"

"Oh yes, it's real. I've read it. He wants to meet you, Mr. President."

"When?"

"Right now. He's already there."

JOHN WASN'T sure what he expected, but it certainly wasn't the man who opened the door.

A black man about 15 years older than John opened the door. He wore a black suit, and had a neatly trimmed gray beard and creases on his skin from smiling.

"Mr. President," the man said with reverence and waited for John to welcome him.

John stood up from his seat and gestured toward the chair in front of him. "Come on in. Take a seat. What's your name?"

He spoke while he moved to the chair. "Jeremiah Stanton. Keeper of the book." He drew it out of his jacket and placed it on the desk. "Normally it stays safe in a suitcase, but I don't like to bring it in that way."

It wasn't any more than a simple leather covered book with aged pages. There wasn't even a design on the front.

"What is that exactly?" John asked without touching it.

"The Book of Secrets." Jeremiah winced slightly as he took a seat, his old bones cracked. "Passed down from president to president. It's not all original. It had been lost sometime during the Civil War, and when it was recovered President Lincoln had it rebound and established the Keepers to see over it." He smiled. "Written by those of your office for those of your office. A few others have read it, such as myself, but not many." Jeremiah nodded his head. "I'm here to explain the parts that may be difficult to understand, as is my job, but I believe you will get most of it on your own."

John still didn't touch it. "What's in it?"

"Everything." Jeremiah's eyes were soft. "The *real* size of the national debt. Who actually killed Lincoln. JFK's dark war. The occult rituals and sacrifices performed within the halls of the White House along with the sequential holy purification to cleanse the dark spirits. The real reasons why we can't leave the Middle East, and why the presidents have chosen to spread the idea that it's about oil." Jeremiah reached down and picked the book up again. "*Everything*. It's all here. All the blood, and all the soul. Every dark bargain, and honored secret. The good and the bad. It's all in there. And it's all yours now." He offered it to John.

With some reluctance, John took the book and opened the cover at some random place in the beginning. Just at a glance he could see that

Thomas Jefferson's name was at the top and there were old drawings of Native American symbols.

Jeremiah cleared his throat and went on as John looked at the book. "Some have noticed that a man will make a great many promises when running for office, some of those men even had certain track records that lent themselves to those promises, but when they assume the presidency they carry out very similar policies as their predecessors. It might be that the small details in social policy change, or something else here or there, but it's all largely the same. Some would speculate that it's all smoke and mirrors, or that there's corruption involved, or something like the deep state controls the office, but none of that is true." Jeremiah pointed at the book. "That's why. When you read it, you'll understand why some presidents entered into costly wars, or why they never followed through on their policy promises. You'll understand why they did it, and why you have to maintain it." Jeremiah took a deep breath and leaned back in his seat.

"That's a lot to take in." John closed the book and sat it on his desk.

"It is. But, Mr. President, that leaves us with the final question." He slid on his warm smile. "When would you like to begin?"

4

"COME ON," Marat begged as he stood at the edge of a tree line. He glanced back to the two women in the car, but no one was looking at him.

It didn't matter. He *felt like* someone was looking at him.

Moments ago, he felt like his bladder was about to burst, now he couldn't piss to save his life.

"*Come on,*" he said with more insistence as he shook himself. He let out a sigh and pulled his pants back up. He dug a cigarette out of his pocket and lit it with an electro lighter he'd found in the car they'd stolen.

Relax. Just be easy and let it go.

That was the problem. Too tense. All he needed was a cigarette and to let his body ease up then he could piss.

He plugged the cigarette into his mouth and looked back at the car.

Moller was looking at him now.

He grinned and held a finger up to her, she nodded and looked away.

The other woman—Winters—was passed out in the back of the car.

After they dragged themselves out of the station, they narrowly made it into the parking lot. The aliens had spread from the station and were heading into the city.

It was a horror show.

Marat tightened his eyes closed and shook his head.

There was no use in replaying all of that in his head. Not if he had any hopes of taking a piss right now.

Alice hadn't been on her feet for more than a few minutes before she completely passed out. Marat was sure she was dead, but Moller was just as confident that she was alive.

They piled Alice into the back of a car and Moller was able to use one of her communication devices to trick the car into starting.

Then the gorgeous blonde woman had looked at him and asked, "You can drive can't you? I never have. All the cars in the United States are automated."

Marat bobbed his head and it wasn't minutes later that they were on the road.

He'd learned to drive back in his teen years before the rail systems were in full effect. These days the roads were mostly barren as any real travel was done on the trains.

But not now. Cars were out driving everywhere. The creatures had spread on the rail lines, and the few that had cars got into them and started driving. Everyone was looking for somewhere else to go, but that wasn't Marat's current problem.

His was a bladder that refused to relax.

"*Shit*," he hissed and pulled his pants down again.

He puffed away at the cigarette and tried not to think that no matter how fast they were in the damn car, the rail systems were faster, and if the creatures were on them, then they'd be in practically every corner of the Soviet Union.

And Marat had personally seen how quickly the monsters spread.

"*Here's the plan*," Moller had told him. "I think I can signal American forces, but we're going to have to get closer and we're going to need a powerful enough transponder. Do you know of any place from here to the German border that we can get to?"

Marat had grinned and nodded. *"Yes, yes of course."*

He didn't know shit.

Marat wasn't a communications officer. He was a programmer. He'd told her that he knew of a place, because what else could he tell the person with the gun in the middle of an alien invasion?

"Yes, of course," he'd repeated.

"Where?"

That was the obvious follow up.

"Uhh. . ." He'd looked like an idiot after that.

She hadn't given him a hard time after that. But why had he even said he knew? What was the point? All he did was—

Wait.

Marat's eyes flared open and the cigarette dropped from his mouth.

There was a propaganda signal center in East Germany where they used to broadcast messages into the West. Marat wasn't sure but he believed it had been decommissioned as a military outlet, but was still in some use. The only reason he knew of it at all was that he heard about it as a case study in university about computer systems.

Now getting inside the damn place might be another thing entirely but at least now he had an idea. He had to—

He just realized he was pissing now and it was rolling to his foot.

"Son of a bitch!"

MOLLER STRAIGHTENED HER LEG, but the CAG caught, making the movement rough.

"Dammit," she whispered. She glanced into the back seat to see Alice still passed out. Moller had taken off Alice's helmet, and now she was drenching the car seat with sweat.

She had been out for hours already with only the occasional mumble.

From the best Moller could tell, Alice looked like she was fine, but that didn't explain the exhaustion or the sweat. Moller knew basic first aid, but Alice was the medical expert.

"What if she loses her mind and becomes like them?" an echo of the last conversation Moller had with Roles.

"Then we'll kill her."

After they'd placed Alice down and Moller took her helmet off, Alice's eyes dilated and she had a distant stare like she wasn't there anymore.

She'll wake up.

Moller had to trust in that.

When she looked back toward Marat he was quickly approaching the car with a massive grin on his face.

"I know good place! We signal your friends." He opened the door and jumped in. "Now we can *fuck* Dodge," he said, still grinning.

"What?" Moller frowned.

"We *fuck* dodge now!"

"I think you mean get the hell out of Dodge."

"Now we get the hell out of Dodge!" Marat thrust a finger up.

Moller couldn't help but grin.

WHEN ALICE KILLED THE HARBINGER, her mind had clung to it in the hive mind. She ripped apart its connections to the other cronux, but when she did, she'd twined her consciousness with it, and when it died, it took a piece of her with it.

She'd pulled back and gotten whiplash and her body shut down.

Now she was floating in the shallows of the hive mind. Its inky blackness ran across her flesh and her mind struggled to reconnect.

"Alice, can you hear me?"

She recognized the voice, but it wasn't real.

"Can you hear me?"

"Yes." It wasn't real but she answered it anyway.

That gave her form.

"It's inside you, Alice, it's eating you from the inside. You're going to be like one of them."

"One of what? Where am I?"

The darkness chilled and her flesh prickled.

"You have to pull back. You're going too deep. Anymore and you'll drown."

"Who are you?"

"They killed me Alice. Don't let them kill you."

"Tommy? Oh my God, Tommy is that you?"

Alice shifted and saw Tommy's cold dead eyes staring at her.

"Don't let them kill our son."

ALICE WOKE in a startle as the car started thumping on an uneven road.

Moller glanced back at her, "Hey, she's—"

"Where are we? What's going on?" Alice glanced around confused.

Moller turned around in the seat to face her. "We're heading to East Germany, do you remember where you are?"

Alice glanced from side to side as everything started to come back. "Yeah, yeah I remember. Do we have any water?"

Moller screwed the top of a bottle and handed it back to Alice who guzzled it down while Moller kept talking. "We have to pull off. We're running out of gas. Marat's going down to a station there and try to refuel the car. You and I have to wait. Not worth letting people see a few Americans in CAG."

Alice rubbed the sweat off her forehead with the back of her wrist and waited until the car pulled over.

When they stopped, Moller looked at Marat. "You going to be okay?"

Marat plastered on a fake grin but gave a thumbs up. "Get fuel. Come back. Very easy."

"Very easy," Moller agreed and gave him a pat on the shoulder. "We'll wait right over there, don't be long."

Alice grabbed her rifle and stepped out of the car. Her legs felt weak, but she wasn't worried about passing out again. They'd pulled off the road and were in some brush. It was lightly coated with snow but warm enough that Alice didn't have to put her helmet back on.

"He said it could be a bit. The station isn't all that close," Moller said as she looked down the dirt road Marat went.

"I'm sure he'll be back soon." Alice walked over to a fallen tree and sat down.

Moller moved over to Alice. "How many do you think there are now?"

"More than we can imagine. Cities full of them. Somehow they got onto the train system. They're going to swallow the Soviet Union whole."

"Hell of a way to win the Cold War." Moller fished out some protein bars from her pack and handed one to Alice. The two sat there quietly eating for a few minutes before Moller spoke. "What was it like having them in your head?"

Alice frowned at the question. Not because she was insulted, but because she didn't know how to answer it.

"It was like having a thousand voices in your head at once, and all of them speaking at the same time. And then it's. . ." She shook her head, struggling for the words. "It's hard to control how you feel."

"What do you mean?" Moller bit off a piece of the bar and chewed.

"I mean, I don't feel like *me*. I feel like *them*."

Moller nodded, but Alice knew she didn't understand. There was no way she could. But she cast a sympathetic look to Alice. "Sounds horrible."

"It is."

They finished their protein bars in silence.

After a time, Alice stood up. It had been long enough and Marat was sure to be back soon. "We're not going to be able to drive all the way to the border. These roads between the Ukraine and Poland are sparse, but the German roads won't be."

Moller shook her head. "If we can get to a radio tower, I think we can send a signal through and see if we can get a pickup, but it'll have to be close. We're going to get to the border and hoof it into Germany. Marat says he knows of a place we can go."

Alice nodded. She didn't have a better plan. "We're going to have a problem though."

"Other than the soldiers and cronux?" Moller half snorted.

"Germany's irradiated." Alice tipped her chin. "Marat doesn't have a suit."

5

JAPANESE TROOP CARRIERS had launched in the seas to land on Soviet territory, chasing the tail of the fleeing Soviet troops. No one had expected the North Japanese to collapse so quickly or for the Soviets to hastily retreat.

New offenses were so quickly enacted that some troops had to be taken on civilian passenger carriers, which now sped through the waters.

Endo was on such a ship.

He paced back and forth. Sitting in place too long made the synthetic intestines hurt. The synthetic organs were designed to move to help the passage of food, but Endo ended up feeling everything slithering around inside his gut, painfully rubbing around in his insides.

As he moved through the bowels of the ship, he saw soldiers sitting in place. Some were recommissioned North Japanese soldiers who were drafted into the ranks of South Japanese, hoping to avoid long prison sentences or execution.

They would soon die regardless.

Endo could tell a soldier's fate by the look in their eyes. One quick glance at a man's face and Endo knew if he would die in war. It was written in their fear.

Sitting there on wood benches beneath the glowing orange light bulbs, Endo knew these men would all be swallowed alive.

They said as much with their whispers, fearful glances, and smells of piss. These men weren't soldiers. They were simply boys thrown into the machine.

Endo's intestines gave a violent twist, but he showed nothing. He moved out of the ship hold and to the upper railing to look over the side.

The doctor had told him the pain could be kept down if he didn't eat too much or too little, but kept a steady supply of soft foods.

Endo pulled out a plastic, tasteless gelatin tube from a belt pouch. It was designed for nutrition and not for enjoyment, and that much was fine. Endo tore the top off with his teeth and squeezed the contents into his mouth. The tasteless white gel slipped down his throat and he placed the wrapper into a belt pouch.

He was supposed to eat them every hour or two for the rest of his life. The doctor had given him advice for when he was sleeping.

"You can slow down when you sleep. Just plan to wake twice to eat it, or you may have severe stomach irritation."

Looking out on the water, he had to wonder if it was all worth it, or if he should jump in and sink to the bottom. Each second he stared the thought became more convincing.

"Endo," Ito's voice growled over the comm link in Endo's ear. *"Report to Command."*

"Confirmed," Endo said, and whatever suicidal thoughts he had drifted away.

He made his way up into a room.

Ito had taken a room with large windows, but he had the shades drawn. Light never suited the man. Some of the other members of *Dark Ocean* were there, five in all with Ito. Each with the red painted claw mark down the faceplate of their helmets.

Ito looked up at Endo as he entered, a cigarette dangling from his mouth.

"Done with your little walking tour?" Ito asked. Endo nodded. "Good. We have plans. We're going to assault a Soviet naval base with a landing force, but our mission is to disrupt the base so more forces can land. From there, *Dark Ocean* is going to break away. We're going to penetrate deeper into the mainland and find out why in hell the Soviets are backtracking so fast."

One of the soldiers, Mori, a man with a shaved head and internal circuitry running across the side of his head from a brain injury, huffed. "They nuked Moscow and there is rioting. It's a collapse. Whole country is falling apart."

Ito exhaled a line of smoke through his nose. "Soviets were putting down dissidents before you were born, Mori. There's more going on than that. We're going to find out and see how best we can kick them in the balls while they're bent over."

Saito, another soldier who always seemed to be grinning, asked, "So we're going in dark and loose? Away from command?"

Ito nodded, and Saito's lips curled into a deeper smile.

Nakamura had a tool out and was using it on his replacement arm, the fine little mechanics in it whirling about as he adjusted them. "I've always wanted to see the Kremlin. I hear it's pretty."

Saito chuckled.

Endo didn't.

Ito ended the meeting and the others moved off. Endo was about to step out again when Ito called him over.

"Endo." Ito's voice was dry.

Endo flashed his eyes toward Ito and saw the man wave him closer. "Come have a drink." He placed two small glasses on a table with peeling white paint near him. Ito poured alcohol into them both and lifted his own, leaving the other for Endo.

"I don't drink."

"You do today." It was all Ito said as he downed the glass and went to fill it again.

Endo took that as a command and grabbed the glass. He looked at it once and then sipped from the glass.

It was strange to drink with a man like Ito, both a military superior and a degenerate. But for all the man's flaws, Ito was a great warrior. Endo had seen him in combat and had followed the man's plans. There was no denying his skill or his strategies.

"You know what your problem is?" Ito said as he filled his own glass.

Endo said nothing, he only sipped.

Ito leaned over and hissed so close that Endo could feel the heat from his rank breath.

"You care too much."

Endo took another sip and looked up now. Ito was staring at him.

"You might be the most dangerous man alive, but you are too much about everything. You need to understand." Ito downed the glass and then slammed it onto the table making it rattle. "*Nothing matters.* There's no point to anything. That's your problem. You want to find the *reason* for things. But there isn't. *Nothing matters,*" Ito repeated. "Do you know how freeing it is to know that? To know that when you kill a man, he doesn't go on to any eternal afterlife. He's simply a body, fit for a hole in the ground. His troubles are over. Ours are over when we die. There is no long judgement or great reward. There's simply *this.*" He held his hand flat toward the ground. "You take what you can and enjoy it while you have it." He shoved a finger at Endo. "Because soon that's all you're going to be. A body for a hole in the ground, and *there's nothing* else after that."

Ito grinned, but his eyes were not kind.

"Let's drink to that." Ito held up his cup.

Endo complied.

THE SOVIET UNION had the largest and most powerful tanks in the world.

Endo knew this from experience.

He'd just seen a shell blow apart a squad of Japanese soldiers in

CAG. All were repurposed North Japanese. Some he'd seen on the ship.

It was their fault.

They shouldn't have clustered.

It was rare for Endo to serve in any kind of massive offensive, or even with the general military, but the attack on the mainland required every bit of help.

The Japanese had moved like a bolt of lightning. There was still fighting in North Japan, but troops were already being gathered and sent after the Soviets. What troops had been captured in South Japan were given a choice.

Join the war or die.

Some North Japanese were already inserted into the Japanese forces.

They of course accounted for the tip of the spear.

They'd gone so fast that they met up with Soviets that were in retreat or were rerouted from Japan.

But the Soviets were not entirely unprepared.

They had tanks deployed around the naval base.

"No! No!" a North Japanese soldier screamed as he clawed at the mud. A Soviet tank rolled forward, its turret turned and looked for a target, much like a dog sniffing a scent. Several Soviet infantry followed alongside it, guns raised and firing at Japanese lines that were breaking from the landing ships.

It rolled right over the screaming soldier.

Endo held still beneath a smoldering Japanese tank and let the enemy roll by.

As soon as it passed, an enemy soldier stepped near. Endo turned the corner and sliced his uranium split blade through the air, dropping the soldier's head. CAG armored infantry took aim at Endo, but he already had his machine pistol up.

Just as the headless soldier fell, Endo pumped several rounds into another enemy's helmet. The first bullet didn't break the CAG, but sent the man reeling back. Two more rounds to the compromised face plate, and one broke through and bounced around inside, shredding the man's brain.

Another soldier let off a burst of rifle fire and Endo jumped onto the tank. Bullets peppered his side and red warnings flashed across his screen, but Endo knew the armor could take a few hits. He let his machine pistol fall loose on its strap and brought the sword up as he moved toward the front of the tank.

Enemy fire forced the Soviet soldiers to take cover behind the tank as it fired. The blast made the whole vehicle jump.

Endo was thrown up and rolled toward the front. He dug his fingers in, desperate for a grip, but slid toward the edge. His foot hooked into a grove just as his helmet hit into the tread.

Khunk-khunk-khunk.

The tracks cracked against his helmet, jittering his head, but he didn't slide under.

Endo grabbed an edge and used it to pull up. Another shot blasted into Endo's side and bounced off harmlessly. There was a dip in the ground and the tank rocked forward, nearly making Endo lose his grip again, but he held tight. He crawled toward the hatch and hammered his sword into the hinge.

Endo grabbed the pommel with both hands and fit his boots into two grooves as he cranked against the hinge.

A normal sword would have broken under such circumstances, but Japanese artisans had designed the uranium split blade to endure the rigors of such force.

The metal hinge cracked and Endo snapped his heel against it to break the rest of the way. He stumbled as his sword came loose, but dug his fingers into the hatch and ripped it open.

He heard men shouting inside as he pulled a frag from his belt and dropped it into the tank. Endo pulled back in enough time to see that a Soviet had climbed onto the tank from the other side, fully armored in CAG. The man fired his rifle at Endo as the grenade went off inside.

The tank kept rolling as Endo darted toward the man, and swung his sword but the man pulled his rifle up and caught it there. Endo gave him a solid kick to the chest and the man fell off the front. His hand dragged across the side and caught hold, but Endo snapped the blade down and took the man's fingers off.

He roared as he fell beneath the still moving tank.

Endo felt nothing. No delight or fear as the dead tank kept lumbering forward.

Japanese forces were destroying Soviet ranks, but Endo knew that this hadn't been a real fight. They'd simply caught up to the troops that had left Japan, and now they killed them for such a retreat.

Wherever the Soviet forces were called too, they weren't going there now. The Japanese had shattered them, and Endo played his part.

Now all that was left was to mop up.

Endo jumped down from the tank and it rolled past. A Soviet soldier who had been escorting it from the other side came around the back and aimed his rifle.

And the world started to lose focus for Endo.

It was one of those moments where his mind became clear and his body distant.

A thought occurred to him and it wasn't the first time.

Why are you doing this?

Was this the will of Heaven? To harry these soldiers and cut them down? To make more widows and fatherless children?

Endo's body moved with mechanical purpose, and he was fast, putting the tip of his sword into the man's throat before he could pull the trigger.

More emptied out of the naval base, but it hardly mattered. He could take each man's measure in a moment—their very movements saying how little they truly knew of war.

He held their lives and weighed them.

They were nothing.

But a new thought occurred.

What if I just let them kill me?

Endo stood and lifted his arms. The soldiers fired and the first few rounds smacked off his armor, but as the shell compromised, the bullets penetrated. They blew in through the shattered chest armor and bounced around through his internals ricocheting off the insides of the armor.

The bullets mutilated him enough that there was nothing left to save, no hope of taking him back and pulling his stomach out and sending him back to war.

He was dead and left in the mud on the battlefield, only to be gathered and thrown into a pit.

But none of that actually happened.

For Endo was hardly a man, but a force of war, and to stand and die was beyond his abilities.

He moved with purpose, his limbs electrified with countless hours of training and seasoned with experience.

They fired at him but he moved in ways that left the eye blind and the hand too slow to aim.

And before they understood that he was a man that could not be killed, he was already upon them, his sword heavy with their blood.

"Kill him! Kill him!"

"Get back!"

"Frag the bastard!"

Endo heard and understood each word, as he spoke Russian perfectly. He heard their cries as he hacked them apart and destroyed their bodies.

Endo only came out of the blur to find a man on the ground with one hand up in surrender, the other a stump upon the ground.

Endo had to wonder what the man's eyes would look like, because he couldn't see them through the CAG helmet.

The man pleaded in Russian, "Please, no!"

Endo shoved the tip of his sword through the man's helmet and pierced his brain, because it didn't matter. The man's life didn't matter.

No one's did. . .

Least of all Endo's.

He ground his teeth as he pulled the sword out, it dragged the man's head with it before it came loose and his body slapped into the ground. The dead man shook as his life seeped out the wound in his head.

Endo didn't want to live anymore. There was no purpose but to make others suffer and die.

"Kill me," Endo whispered inside the helmet.

There was more shouting but he barely heard it. Japanese troops were moving near him preparing to enter the naval base while Soviet soldiers fired from fortifications.

The war continued as Endo stood in place.

"Kill me." He pressed the clasp on his helmet and it came loose.

"Disengaged. Disengaged. Disengaged." His helmet warned over and over as he pulled it off and dropped it.

Endo didn't want to live anymore. Not with the synthetic organs sliding around in his stomach, painfully rubbing his insides.

Not for this.

Endo walked through the paved roads inside the base and toward the communications structure as shots fired past him. Large pillars near the entrance provided cover and a Soviet soldier peeked out from behind one. Endo held his arms out to his side, still gripping the pommel of his sword.

"Kill me!" Endo yelled in Russian.

The confused soldier shifted back behind the cover.

"Kill me!" he raged and went around the side.

The soldier brought his gun up, and Endo hacked the barrel and stock, catching the tips of the man's fingers. The man roared with pain and fired a round. It blew out awkwardly from the damage to the rifle and Endo dodged low.

Endo stepped onto the man's armored fingers on the ground and jolted forward to slash the sword across the man's helmet. It left a groove and shot out sparks, but it didn't go through.

The cut must have damaged the cameras on the helmet as the man's head started to whip around as if unable to see.

"Kill me!" Endo slashed again, and left another groove.

A shell from Japanese artillery smashed down dangerously close and threw debris up into the air. Endo stumbled back as he blocked it from his eyes. As he came up, there was a thick smoke choking the air. A second soldier came over a downed wall from the base and aimed at Endo. He fired a blast off and Endo ducked low and the bullets smashed into the bricks behind him. He moved low and came up underneath the man's arms, whipping the sword to take the man's right arm below the elbow.

Endo kicked him in the chest and the man fell back as blood surged from his arm.

No one can do it.

The realization hit Endo.

Another soldier shot at him from inside the dark base. The electricity had gone out and the lights had died, sun beamed light through holes in the wall. Endo stepped inside as the soldier back tracked and fired at him.

Endo shifted his weight low and raced forward.

By instinct alone, Endo knew where the bullets were and he moved from their path, bending and shifting his stance to pass each.

He wanted to die, but decades of training and raw instinct made it impossible to surrender.

One of the soldier's bullets smacked off of Endo's shoulder, but none made it close to his head. He lept into the air and crashed into the soldier.

They tumbled onto the ground and Endo came up on top. The man's hand reached up but Endo whipped his sword and took it off at the wrist.

The man beat at him as Endo stared down. The soldier's one good hand grabbed at Endo's arm and tried to shake him away but Endo reached up for the clasp below the man's helmet where the release was.

Endo pressed it and the helmet popped off unsealed and came loose.

The gray haired snarling man shouted curses as Endo fit his hands across the man's neck, crushing in the armor.

Grinding his teeth together, Endo pressed tightly, watching the man sputter and die.

More people shouted deeper inside the base and Endo turned upright in a blood lust.

He shouted as he moved in their direction.

"Kill me!"

6

SERGEI GARIN STEPPED into the small broadcasting booth as his officers watched on. The whole room was in a dreadful silence.

The door shut behind him.

The small booth with its noise-cancelling walls and a single microphone wasn't military, but it could broadcast on their signals.

All that remained of the Soviet Union would hear his words.

He was a gray-haired man with many years behind him. There had been many challenges in Garin's life.

But nothing could have prepared him for this.

He distinctly remembered the day he'd become a man. He'd woken that morning long ago as a boy of twelve and found out that his father's fever had grown all the worse.

You have to break the soil," his father, burning with sickness, had told him. *"Break it before the frost comes in tonight or you won't have a crop come spring."*

His father died a few hours later. Sergei Garin and his two sisters wrapped their father in a rug and placed him in the woods.

By night time, Garin was sure the wolves would be at his father's body, but it didn't matter.

There hadn't been time to bury him.

Not if they wanted a crop in spring.

His father would have understood.

He wanted them to break the soil.

He woke up that day as a boy of twelve and ended that day as a man of twelve.

Life had been long and hard, but through it all, he'd always seen himself the same way.

He was a farmer's son.

He still was, though now his voice was rough as he spoke to all that remained of the Russian people. "This is Sergei Garin. Major General of the Second Guards Red Army. This signal is broadcasting on all available civilian and military channels."

His actions would be tantamount to treason, but Moscow had gone silent, and the Soviet Union was burning.

The people needed a voice.

He would be that voice.

"Until further notice, I am assuming command as grand marshal of the Soviet military and relocating the capital to Leningrad."

He didn't look back at his officers.

They too were now traitors.

"A dangerous enemy has set upon us."

His voice was stiff. Resolute.

His life had led him to this point.

"These orders are for both civilian and military alike. Those near Leningrad should make their way here or to Berlin, which has been confirmed as secure. But beware, the roads are treacherous and the enemy has taken our rail systems to spread throughout our union. Those incapable of making it to a safe region should form pockets of resistance to combat the menace and survive so that we may rebuild. Disable or destroy nearby rail systems, seek shelter, and trust in your blood. We are a strong people."

Garin took a deep breath, and when he spoke now it was earnest. "We will survive. We will live on. We will rebuild." He took another breath and waited a moment. "Standby for further instructions."

He turned and exited the booth, one of his officers went inside and pulled the door closed so that they could transmit more of what they knew to the population.

Garin looked each of his officers in the face, looking for doubt or dissatisfaction.

They were all good soldiers, but a good soldier should have marshaled the men under his command and set off to restore the capital.

But Garin wasn't quite a good soldier.

He was a farmer's son.

When hell opened upon the Soviet Union, Moscow had ordered the Second Guards Red Army to hold the line should European forces invade. It wasn't much longer after that when orders came in to instead head east to fight the enemy besieging Moscow.

But their military trains were no longer working. They had become entirely disrupted.

There were other systems that seemed functional, but those that Garin needed were inoperable. He set his technicians to work on them, but Moscow fell before anything could be done.

Against the Nazi invasion, the Russian people had lasted for months.

But now, against these horrors, Moscow had fallen in days.

Worse still, the reports were that they were emitting from a black site bunker east of Moscow.

Garin could have gathered his forces and fit those that he could into their trucks and tanks and headed off to fight, but with no further contact with command, he decided he would fortify Leningrad to protect the civilian population and prepare for a counter attack.

Some might have called it cowardice. Garin would have called it practical.

Along with his team of officers, Garin stood in front of a digital map of Leningrad.

"Situation report," he barked.

His officers gave him a string of reports ranging on everything from barrier construction, refugee processing, and the destruction of the rail systems. They even told him of his access to a few still operational short-ranged missiles—phantom-class nukes.

But then there were the rumors coming in about America.

Were they to blame? Did they unleash this hell upon the Soviet people?

And what of the reports that the American president was killed by a Soviet assassin?

Garin didn't doubt the reports, though he wasn't privy to such knowledge. Either way, such things were not his concern at the moment.

"Sir!" A fully armored soldier interrupted the briefing. "Scouts have reported, a mass of the creatures are on their way here."

Garin leaned up from the table. "How long do we have?"

"A few hours at most."

Garin looked at his officers. "You all know what to do. We may be the last remaining sizable Soviet force. Hold the line." The officers filed out. Garin pointed at one of his officers. "You, come here."

"Help me with my CAG."

———

THE LIFE of a hatchling was not particularly complex. A being, typically a Harbinger, chewed up meat and regurgitated it into the open flaps of the egg.

When that DNA collected into a stew, the hatchling began to take shape. When he'd grown to an appropriate size and shape, the hatchling would claw out of the fleshy folds of his egg, his naked body steaming with heat, and eat what remained of the egg.

If the clutch had any brothers or sisters with imperfections, they too would be eaten.

Such was the way of things.

One hatchling in particular knew his name before he'd ever taken his first breath. The name had been buried within the stew, and it had shaped inside the growing creature.

The hatchling, Davin, had mumbled his name while he formed, sending out tiny bubbles though his pink lips.

In time, the egg began to shrivel and weaken, and Davin's time had come. He poked his fingers up through the brittle folds of the egg. He peeled back the skin and stuck his arms into open air.

He clawed out of the egg, a naked and steaming thing in the cold air.

Being a hatchling, he was not as strong as other members of his race, and he grew cold quickly.

Another near him had crawled out of its egg. It moaned loudly and puked up foam as Davin moved past it.

There were few things Davin understood, but he obeyed the commands of his instincts. He went to the pile of crumpled clothes near the wall.

"*Suhnny day,*" one of his wide eyed brothers moaned despite being in a dark basement with no view of the sky. "*Suhnny day.*"

Davin paid him no mind as he struggled into the clothes. His limbs were still weak and soft, though they would harden in time.

"*They dun know.*" Another raspy voice from a brother with long, ragged hair. He shook his head and walked in a circle as he shivered, repeating the same useless phrase over and over. A strange combination of memories not quite formed while in the egg.

The last of the clutch was a human woman, and she spoke with a scratch in her voice, puking up raw excess tissue with each word. "*Ward. . . I wok. . . Ward.*" She bent over and hacked up everything to clear her throat. "*I work in the ward.*" She whispered the words but they were clear.

Now it was Davin's turn, and his mind struggled for thoughts. "*Dab-in,*" he choked out the word, gurgling excess flesh from his throat. He spit out a mouthful. "Davin. My name is Davin."

Just as the others, those words meant nothing to him. They were simply memories that had been sewn into him.

"My name is Davin," he repeated.

His words mixed in with the other hatchlings as they all began to dress.

"Factory manufacturing and—"

"—Ukranian junction of—"

"—my son is—"

Each was speaking the words that had somehow come to them. Most were likely useless. Simple programming.

"My name is—"

Davin droned as he fit his boots on.

And each time he spoke.

"... is Davin."

His words became clearer.

"—name—"

Shaper.

"My name—"

More human.

"—is Davin."

He then left the safety of the cold room for the upper floor of the house.

Where was he? Who had put him there?

None of this was a concern. None of it was important.

He walked past screaming people as cronux thrashed their bodies. Some even called for his help, apparently surprised at his presence. "My name is Davin," he said to one screaming woman as she reached for him.

This small town was burning, and though he was still hungry, it was not for him to feed upon any there.

Instinct drove him elsewhere.

He walked for hours or possibly days, he wasn't sure how long as he didn't have a particularly strong concept of distance or time. He felt a pull in one direction with whispers from the hive mind, so he went that way.

A crowd of humans were lining up to enter a city.

"My name is—"

He spoke the words to no one in particular as he lined up within the crowd, moving when they moved and stopping when they stopped.

An old man tugged at his sleeve. Davin turned back to him. The old man mumbled words, but Davin neither understood or cared. "My name is Davin," he said and turned back in line.

As people flowed into the city, there was a checkpoint where soldiers with guns asked questions.

The hatchling was pushed forward. A soldier spoke to him.

"My name is Davin."

The soldier said something else.

"My name is Davin."

The soldier stopped and spoke again.

"My name is—"

The soldier slapped his arm and pointed him away.

Davin went to a cluster of others that had filtered into the city. Each was mewing and crying. He put his back to the wall and slid down to his ass and stared out.

That was all that was needed.

He was an organic time bomb. He simply waited to explode.

GARIN HAD SEEN the creatures himself. Each was a pale eyeless beast, but that was where the commonalities ended. Some were tall and others short and staunch. They had long reaching arms with twisted fingers, or no arms at all but powerful jaws that could snap a man in full CAG in half.

But they'd always been in small groups, easily dispatched by his men.

He was no fool though. He knew what they were.

Scouting parties

But now as his CAG helmet camera processors tightened their telescopic vision, he saw a sea of horrors approaching, and he wasn't sure he could hold them back.

"Is the armored regiment ready?" he asked his officer.

A CAG clad soldier standing nearby with a datapad nodded. "Yes, sir, the tanks are forming in the perimeter, and artillery is prepared to begin its bombardment. Should we engage the warplanes?"

"No." Garin allowed the cameras to unfocus and his vision returned to normal. "The bastards are smart, and there are reports they took down aircraft in Moscow. We need to see what they can do before we order out our weapons. Begin the artillery bombardment."

Normally he would have aerial sight with imaging from satellites and the Soviet moon base, but it had all gone dark for reasons he didn't know. Garin turned away and stiffened his spine. He folded his hands behind his back.

For all the stern and confidence that Garin had, there was an uneasy feeling crawling around in the pit of his stomach, just as when he and his sisters had wrapped his father up and left him in the woods.

Decisions were going to be made soon.

Painful decisions.

IN THE DISTANCE, somewhere in the city, loud booms made everyone near Davin panic and squirm. They jumped with each blast.

Not Davin. He had slumped against the wall and slid down it, his eyes gazing away at nothing particular. Some had tried to talk to him, but they all eventually left him alone when he didn't speak.

Though his body was in the city, his mind wasn't.

It was in the horde, joined with each of his brothers.

He felt their rumbling presence. Some had walked all the way from Moscow, while others had emptied out of trains, and all joined within the horde.

An army for the one god of this world.

The scarred Archon.

His was a mind unlike any other, and his thoughts flowed to each of them.

And now the Archon spoke, to him, an echo from within the hive mind.

Now.

Davin leapt to his feet. His mind snapped into focus. He roared as tentacles burst from his body. Those around him scattered.

A blood-soaked tendril pierced into a screaming man and pulled him in. The weight unbalanced Davin, and he fell to the ground as the man was pulled in. Davin sank his teeth into the man's throat and a parasite spewed out of his mouth.

Davin went to his feet even as the parasite dug into the man's neck, making him rattle around on the floor.

The crowds screamed and separated, but Davin's tentacles snatched around a woman's throat. He spat a parasite into her ear.

The tiny white creature's tendrils thrashed in the air as it looped around the woman's ear.

She backpedaled and tripped over the man on the ground as she fought to rip it off.

The deceptively strong tendrils went down her ear canal and pulled the fat parasite in as the woman howled in pain.

Davin's jaws stretched open inhumanly wide. Skin tore in the corners. The flesh under his eyes sagged, and crawling cronux musculature squirmed in the pink beneath.

Just as Davin reached for the next person, his arms cracked and popped, elongating. The man he'd bitten was already beginning to stand, a fresh soldier for the hive mind.

But even with his lips wet with blood and the people near him roaring, a strange loop played through Davin's head.

"My name—" He spat blood as tiny tentacles reached out through his mouth. "—*is Davin.*"

GARIN HAD GOTTEN a report that there was rioting in the civilian processing center. He sent a team down to put a stop to things.

His helmet's camera processors tightened once more, and he saw the artillery blowing apart the creatures.

Perhaps he had misjudged them. Maybe they weren't as intelligent as he suspected, as this horde of dumb beasts seemed to come directly into fire, but were easily held back with artillery.

The shelling blasted them apart, and what little got through was quickly cut down by tanks and infantry fire. There were already dark clouds forming in the sky from the flame troopers setting so many of their corpses on fire.

The city was not set up for war footing, and the booming artillery was close enough that it could seriously damage the hearing of any civilian, so they were kept in another district.

But the CAG armor damped such noise, and Garin had no problem with the blasts of the weapons.

"Sir!" a message came through his helmet comms. "It's not a riot! The creatures have gotten inside. They're spreading among the civilians! They're headed toward the artillery!"

In a flash, Garin imagined the monsters falling upon his heavy weapons and the blasts going silent.

He turned to glance out toward the field.

Nothing would stop the sizable force from swooping down on the city and extinguishing what was left of the Soviet forces.

Garin began moving and his officers followed behind him.

"Rifle!" he barked at a man who threw him one. He looked at Nikitin. "With me"

"Sir?"

"If they destroy the artillery, we will lose Leningrad."

THE ARCHON WALKED FORWARD. The grass beneath his feet curled and darkened from his radiation.

Once-men flowed around the Archon. They walked awkwardly on broken and malformed legs while powerful cronux stayed back and waited for the lines to soften.

An artillery shell landed close by and disintegrated the bodies of his children.

But the scarred Archon remained unconcerned. Their purpose was to die. They would absorb the bombardment.

They were only a distraction.

His children on the inside would be what brought the city down.

Now.

He sent the command through the hive mind, and all came up at once.

Powerful beast, yet unseen by the enemy, crawled up from behind the hills and trees beyond the battlefield and raged forward.

These cronux had come through the gate, and they had been crafted and bred for war.

One such beast, with legs as thick as logs, braved forward. Its jaws were large enough to swallow a car, and when it roared, it could be heard from miles away.

Kill.

The Archon saw it storm forward amidst the explosions on the ground and snap hold of a man, swallowing him in a single bite.

Others followed. Some did not fare as well, but all fought. A tank shell smashed into one powerful beast and blew out its insides. It lazed up onto three feet and dragged a broken leg behind it as it continued on.

The Archon watched as his forces flowed into the tanks and shredded them. A long legged cronux stretched up as a shell fired through its legs. It came down onto the tank and forced its thin fingers into the hatch. It peeled it open with a grunt while its teeth snapped. Smaller brothers flowed up over the tank and into the hole. The men inside were eaten alive.

The Archon kept a lazy walk forward until he had nearly made it to the city entrance. He walked past the broken tanks and screaming men dying inside them.

There were still lines of soldiers firing, but the Archon's children careened into the encampments. The lines broke and cronux shredded men while other men fired and some retreated.

A man turned to run only to have his foot snatched out from under him, a cronux dragging him off.

Another fired as he dragged away a wounded comrade, but the injured soldier succumbed to the parasite and grabbed his ally, bringing him down to the ground to gnaw his throat. Other men fought bitterly as they were overwhelmed, firing all the ammunition they had. A few men took their own lives with a shot to the head.

This war was an easy one. There was little in the way of tactics or concern, but only brute force to crush the enemy.

The Archon desired a challenge.

Did this world have any to offer?

GARIN HAD SO few men left that he joined the rifle teams as they moved to cut off the creatures. Garin went shoulder to shoulder behind an overturned food stand with his men and unleashed on the oncoming creatures.

Civilians ran toward them screaming, and some were cut down by jittery soldiers while others were able to make it behind the line.

"Come on, come on!" one soldier said, waving the people through.

A woman came around a building corner and made it only a few feet before the horde flowed out behind her. A wave of creatures, so tightly packed it looked like a single mass of arms and legs, flowed through the streets.

The woman stumbled and had only a moment to scream as they flowed over her.

"Kill them!" Garin shouted into the comms.

Rifle fire came from all corners of the street and from teams placed up in buildings, firing down from windows. They rained down on the creatures, but for everyone that collapsed, there were others to step over the bodies.

Artillery fire boomed overhead.

"Flame troopers!" Garin ordered.

Heavy armored troopers stormed forward, shoulder to shoulder, and let loose a kiss of flame.

The fire blasted out and melted the screaming monsters.

Even through the dark, smoky haze, Garin could see the mouths of the melting creatures roaring as they sizzled, burned, and collapsed. But even in those dying moments, they were still reaching for the men and still stepping forward until their bodies gave way.

There were more, so many more, and the lines of battle were stretching across multiple locations.

But Garin had hoped that here would be the place where they drew their line and forced the creatures back. That this would be the place where the Soviet resistance would begin and that there would be no end of his people or culture.

That they all would survive for another day.

Then a message came in. *"Sir! The front lines are breaking! They're destroying the tanks!"*

THOUGH THE ARCHON was not in the city, he saw his children burn and collapse, for he had many eyes in this world.

The powerful weapons of man still rained down on his children, and many great beasts died.

The resistance of these men was strong, but Archon craved such games.

He would see how they would do with a new challenge.

When the Mother had given him life, she'd given him purpose to take the world and reshape it.

He had done so.

There were other things of this world beyond man, and the Archon had so many wonderful ideas for them.

He looked back to the woods and pointed a single long finger. He gestured toward the city.

Thousands of dark wings filled the air. They cawed as they took flight.

There was no precise command for which they should target, but only a simple order.

Kill.

Despite all the firepower, Garin's forces were driven back. He had Nikitin order a direct shelling inside the city to bring down one of the buildings for further cover. A dangerous gamble this close to his men and with the enemy bearing down on them, but it was needed.

After surrendering so much ground, he was able to reposition his forces at a choke point between broken cars and a narrow road that the creatures funneled into.

With the battlefield tightened, the flame soldiers became all the more effective with crossing zones of fire. Dark clouds from all the burning flesh choked the sky.

"Sir!" One of Garin's men pointed up.

A cloud was swirling, and then a strange blackness flowed through like it had sprung a leak. It twisted and turned in the sky before diving down on the flame soldiers.

Birds.

Waves of beaks and feathers coated the flame soldiers, so many at once that a hundred pecking beaks cracked the armor.

"Above! Above! Get the flames above!" Garin shouted.

One of the hoses snapped on the soldier and he exploded, throwing armor and meat in all directions and killing all his attackers too.

The confusion and gap in the line was all that was needed for the once-men to flow through. Their cooking fingers grabbed onto flame soldiers as their charred tentacles wrapped around them, sucking them into the horde.

One flame soldier turned his weapon up and burst the fire into screeching birds, turning them into nothing more than burnt bodies slapping the ground. The man, his torch still pointed up, was overwhelmed by creatures on the ground and dragged down. His screams were heard on the comms until Garin cut his transmission.

The birds swam into the air and moved overheard toward the artillery placements.

Soon they would fall upon the heavy weapons, and the frontal attacking forces would have no resistance.

The battle was lost.

Screams and calls for help blasted over the comms, but Garin flipped those off too.

He entered the commands on his comms to be placed over all frequencies and to be heard by all men.

"I am ordering a retreat toward the docks. All civilians are to be hastily checked. Any with wounds are to be executed and thrown into the sea. All aid equipment is to be moved on ship." He took a moment to breathe. "We are leaving Leningrad." He ended the frequency and dialed in the frequency on the Missile Combat Crew.

"Lieutenant," he barked into the comms.

"*Yes, sir!*" a man responded.

"Do we still have access with our missile payloads?"

"Yes, sir," the man said once more.

"Dial in the black site bunker east of Moscow. Unload everything."

7

A SMALL LINE of soldiers stayed behind to keep the Archon from destroying the army in Leningrad. They held off as the others left on ships, but those last defenders were soon overwhelmed.

The Archon himself had dragged the commander of the men up the stairs of a building and onto the roof.

Why did he do it? What was the purpose? Perhaps there wasn't one.

He simply desired it.

The Archon had held the man by the throat and peeled his helmet off as he lifted the man over the edge of the building.

The man's eyes were angry and hateful.

It had been enjoyable.

The man cursed and kicked, but it had all been useless.

The Archon barely listened. Instead he whispered into the hive mind.

Come.

A dark swarming cloud of birds swam in the air.

They dove down and pecked the man's flesh.

The man raged within the Archon's grasp.

And then all at once, the Archon's mind flashed with terrible pain.

Gone. Sucked into the void.

For the briefest of moments, the gate, far away from where he was now, had collapsed. It cut his presence with the Mother.

He went mad.

The Archon threw his head back and roared so loudly, the cronux near him shrank back or ran away in fear.

A dizzying fit of anger came over him and threw the man into the air, hurling him some great distance, and the birds followed.

Just as the man cracked into the side of some building, the Archon lost his footing and fell from the roof.

He had no fear or concern.

Only anger from losing his connection with the Mother.

There was an intense impact as he smashed into the ground. The force did not hurt him, but it killed the cronux he landed on.

The Archon leaned up, and the pale body he landed on quivered and shook.

He slashed his hand down and ripped off its head to hurl off in the distance. Near him others shrieked and fled.

"Mother!" the Archon screeched.

He went into the hive mind and reached for his gate. It was gone. Something had destroyed it.

But he could not be without her.

He fell to his knees as his children around him screamed in misery and pain, their suffering flowing from the Archon.

He stepped fully into the hive mind.

It was dark and cold.

Quiet.

One of his children came up with a shrill voice, howling because it felt the desolation of the Archon.

He reached over and snuffed its life.

He desired silence, and the hive mind became a place of quiet.

There was another gate. He knew it. Where was it?

Just as the Jade Archon had reached out, now so did the scarred Archon.

There in the distance he saw it. A pinprick of a gate. . . His brother had already come through.

But there was another.

It was far, but closer than the Jade Archon. They were building a gate there for his second brother.

He would be here soon.

The Archon pulled back from the cold chambers of the hive mind, but he looked for a human name for that place.

Iran.

He needed to be quick. He would go and take the gate while his children continued to spread the faith.

He called forth a leader within his army, one of his Janissaries.

"Go," the Archon told him, even as he called others to travel with him to Iran.

The scarred Archon had wanted a challenge, hadn't he?

Three Kings.

Three crowns.

Three to rule the world.

But why need there be three when one would suffice?

8

MILES HAD BEEN in a lot of places and had done a lot of disgusting things. He once did a show where a man fried up cow intestine and ate it as a way to cure his erection problem. Miles had taken a bite himself, grabbed his crotch, and given a thumbs up to the camera.

"It works!"

The audience loved it.

He'd also visited the small village out in some godforsaken country where the dead supposedly could get up and walk. In reality, it was just the town's local spirit guide dancing with corpses. Pretty disgusting, though it had made for good TV.

But this was something else entirely.

Rat had taken them across the city, and while it seemed true that the largest mass of creatures had moved out, there were still small groups hunting.

Packs of three or more at a time moved like hunched demons, seemingly always in a hurry as they stopped, inspected the area, and then tore off in dead sprints.

They even saw other humans. A woman and her daughter came out onto the road. Rat waved at them, but they ran off, too afraid to approach anyone.

Miles was beginning to think they'd get all the way through without a problem when Rat hissed at them and waved his hand low to the ground.

Miles dropped low behind a car near Kevin when he caught sight of a pack racing up the street. He held his breath and closed his eyes, willing his heart to stop beating for fear of the sound. When he opened his eyes he saw both Kevin and Rat flat against the ground and half underneath the car, so Miles flattened down next to them to get a good view.

The creatures had taken pause in the center of the street. One was a four-legged thing with a long, stretching tongue and an exposed brain. Its tongue waved around in the air as its head shifted from side to side as if trying to find them.

Miles leaned onto his side so he could slide his camera out of his pocket and take aim. He caught sight of Kevin who shook his head but Miles frowned.

What the hell does he think we're here for?

He turned the camera on and started filming.

It was disgusting, though Miles wouldn't have put it in the top ten of his life.

But something else came next.

It had been human once, that was apparent by its rotten legs—something had chewed on them and now the flesh peeled off in chunks—but that was where the similarities ended. From the waist up, it was one big tumor with bubbling sacks of skin.

"Fu. . ."

Miles always felt the need to put on a good face, so he grinned and whispered, *"Looks like my ex-wife."* But he was certain his ass had tightened just as much as Kevin's.

"How can it even see where it's going?" Kevin whispered back.

It was a good question, but Miles didn't have an answer. He only grunted a response.

The creature with the long tongue turned to look at a store front. It pawed over while the walking tumor stumbled and tried hard to keep up on its feet.

The tongued creature leapt forward and smacked against the door. Someone shouted from inside the store front.

"Hell, there are people in there," Miles whispered.

Rat tensed up as if he were getting ready to move. Miles shot him a stiff glance and shook his head.

The creature clawed at the door and smashed it, but the heavy iron doors refused to budge.

It turned its head toward the walking tumor and roared, throwing spittle through its fanged teeth.

With a slow start, the tumor shifted its top-heavy weight and moved in a quick rush toward the door. It hit and blew up slinging fluids and smoke from the combustion. The sudden explosion made Miles wince and he nearly dropped the camera.

"There are people in there! We gotta do something," Kevin hissed.

Rat moved to stand again, but Miles grabbed his sleeve.

"We don't *gotta* do a damn thing." He bared his teeth at Rat and Kevin. "I'm no killer and neither are you. Those people are already dead."

The people screamed and one man rushed toward the open door. He glanced back. The tongue shot out and pierced through his shoulder and dragged him back in.

"Next time, get the good camera out so I don't have to use this piece of shit," Miles said to Kevin as he flipped the handheld camera off and slid it into his pocket. "Come on, let's get the hell out of here before it comes out looking for dessert."

RAT TOOK THEM ON A TWISTING, widening route. Miles marveled as they walked right underneath a sky-high track where he could imagine the trains speeding through. Instead, a single train lazed by and someone, man or woman, he wasn't sure, was screaming on it.

"Lovely," he'd mumbled as it passed.

They had to stop and hide on a few occasions as marauding groups passed. But Miles nearly shit his pants when they came upon someone alone in the street.

A man staggered out of a building clutching his throat. Despite the bastard he was, every instinct told Miles to go see if he could help, but the little voice in his head said otherwise.

Don't move.

He'd learned to trust that voice and they all ducked inside a broken storefront to watch.

The man rolled around on the ground and moaned out words in Russian, though Miles didn't understand it.

"What's he saying?" Kevin whispered.

"Help me." The color drained out of Rat's face.

The man's back arched while he screamed and clawed at his throat.

Miles slapped Kevin's arm and made a camera "click" motion.

With reluctance, Kevin slid the camera out of his bag. "Just feels dirty..." He started filming.

"Dirty pays." Miles felt like a bit of a bastard himself, but that rarely stopped him.

The man in the streets rolled around violently until he went limp.

"Rest in peace." Miles motioned a cross against his chest and was starting to pick his things back up when the man moaned once more and clawed to his feet. The skin on his neck parted as if a seam came loose and a black oily tentacle poked out, stretching several feet in length, far more than Miles ever would have thought possible.

"The bite. It changes them." Rat frowned. "Makes them... strange."

"No kidding," Miles whispered.

They waited in utter silence until the man moved away.

"Sun is going down." Rat pointed. "We should sleep here."

Kevin glanced out the broken storefront. "But there's no door, they could come right in!"

"That is good I think." Rat pointed at his eyes and then at the large apartment buildings. "Many people are still here. Hiding. I see monsters go and break doors. Hunting. We just stay quiet, and they don't look here. I think."

"Hell of a gamble." Miles winced and looked at Kevin.

"He got us this far." Kevin shrugged.

Miles nodded. "Well. . ." He slugged up his bag. "Let's see if there's a nice place to take a piss."

MILES NEARLY SHAT on himself for the second time in twenty-four hours when he woke up with Rat crouching overtop of him.

"Shhh." The scrawny Russian man had a finger to his lips.

Miles gave a slow nod and saw that Kevin was already up and looking out a window.

Miles crawled over. A pack of the creatures was scaling the side of a building as if it were no problem at all. There were still some city lights struggling with life, and they illuminated the creatures as they paused to look into the occasional window.

Miles rubbed his eyes and he could see them more clearly now. Long-jointed legs that bent just like a spider's and wide mouths. Typically the creatures looked different, but these four in particular looked similar.

"What are those bastards doing?" Miles mumbled.

"Hunting," Rat growled.

Kevin whispered, "When the horde left, some of them stayed. They're rooting out survivors. Why would they do that?"

"Isn't that obvious, mate?" Miles said without looking away. "They don't want to leave survivors."

One paused at a window, then it quickly moved around, its head staying in place as the rest of its body shifted. It gasped and the others raced over. With a single powerful leg it smashed the window open and ripped the glass away, then it crawled inside. The others followed.

The lights flipped on and someone started shouting. Moments later a body was flung through the window. Miles watched it come all the way down and smash into the ground. There was more shouting.

It wasn't when the body hit the ground, but only when it started to get back to its feet with dead eyes in its head that Miles finally realized.

This is the ugliest place I've ever been.

Worse than North Japan or tracking the desert skin thieves or any other lowly, horrible place he'd been.

This was the ugliest.

But he smiled, if only because to do anything else would hurt too much, and he looked at Kevin.

"Turn the camera on."

As soon as the sun was up, Miles took his morning piss in the corner of the store and peeked outside.

Certain that there was nothing lurking around any corner, he gave the other two a thumbs up.

"Let's go."

Under Rat's guidance, they swooped to the outskirts of the city and avoided the portion of the city where the nuke dropped. They even came across a few other groups of survivors, but everyone warned them not to go in that direction.

Some man with terrified eyes and a bloody military jacket pointed. After an exchange, Rat came back to Miles.

"He said there is bunker out there. They come from bunker." Rat scowled.

"Well, that's where I want to go, just to get a peek," Miles said.

They left the other group behind and continued on a path, leaving Moscow behind. They headed east until they saw the bunker off in the distance. Miles held up his hand.

"We gotta start rolling here." Outside of a small dirt path, some trees, and melting snow, there wasn't much, but Miles was already rolling the image around in his head. He snapped his fingers a few times and pointed at Rat. "You. Come here. I'm gonna record us talking. Don't worry about the accent, make it thicker. People love it. Now, Kevin, you start rolling and make sure you get these paths in the background, and you keep the whole thing playing so that we can get one of those creatures on camera."

Kevin's voice quivered as he asked, "But what if one of those things gets up close?"

Miles skewed his eyes and glanced over his shoulder. "Well, fuck, I hope you'd tell me if you see one of them sneaking up on me."

Kevin nodded and pulled the camera out of his bag and aimed it as Miles stepped into position.

"Wait!" Miles stopped him to muss his hair up more and undo the top button of his shirt. He poured some water in his hand and splashed it on his face. Kevin only frowned, and Miles motioned for him to begin.

"Hello there, friends," Miles whispered, his eyes deadly serious and focused on the camera. "Welcome to *Westwood's Wild World.*" He paused, and some would have taken it as dramatic, but Miles was actually considering if he was legally allowed to call the show *Westwood's Wild World* as the station owned the rights. It didn't matter. He decided he'd figure it out later and edit it out if need be. "We're here in the heart of the Soviet Union, just outside of Moscow trying to find out the *real story* of what's happening behind the Iron Curtain, and let me tell you friends. . ." Now when he paused, it was for emphasis. Miles tipped his chin down and looked dramatically at the camera, all while Rat stood next to him confused and uncertain. "We've had outworldy visitors. *Aliens.* And our guide here—" Miles slapped Rat on the back. "Is going to—"

"No, no, no!" Rat shook his head and backed away. "I don't want on camera. It's not good. People see me on camera, it's not good."

"Well hell, mate, why didn't you say so?" Miles scoffed. He rolled his finger at Kevin. "Let's start over again. How about you focus on the bunker then cut back? We'll just—"

"Oh shit!" Kevin pointed to something in the distance.

Miles had only a half second to consider as he turned around.

There was a quick flash of light, and he instinctively snapped his eyes closed and put his hand up in front of his face.

A blast wave ripped through the area, and the wave threw Miles into the air.

All at once he couldn't breathe, like a belt was strapped around his neck and tightened. Miles rolled onto his back and gasped open his mouth, but no oxygen came in.

He mouthed like a dying fish as he felt the blood bubble in his head.

I'm going to die here.

That thought came on with strange clarity, and another followed it.

It doesn't matter.

Miles choked and fought for breath, but he was not panicking.

He was okay.

In those final moments, there were strange flashes in his mind of all the horrible things he'd done.

And Shailene, his ex-wife.

He thought of her.

No more running, mate, his thoughts told him.

Cards are flipped.

You're dead.

Couldn't happen to a nicer cunt.

With a sinking calmness, he laid flat on his back. But when he twisted his head . . .

He saw Kevin struggling to breathe, and Rat already face down flat in the dirt.

Fucking hell.

Miles deserved it all and worse.

But the kid, and the scraggly bastard who helped them?

They didn't.

Miles imagined few people in the world were as calm in the face of death. That calm demeanor had certainly helped him get laid a time or two, but in reality.

He just didn't care.

That was a nuke. Not the kind that fries everything, or there wouldn't be any of you left. Instead—

Miles rolled onto his feet and wheezed, only getting sips of air.

—there was a small tactical explosion and it felt like the oxygen had been fried.

He dug his hand into his satchel and looked for his rad pills.

That was a phantom class tactical warhead.

He dug out a pill bottle, his own head swimming.

His vision was starting to haze as he looked over at Kevin, still writhing. Rat, the poor bastard, didn't seem to be moving at all.

Miles popped the pill bottle. He dumped the entire contents into his hands and they spilled out, a few in his palm and the rest across the dirt.

He glanced down at his hand like it betrayed him, but it was growing numb and he was losing feeling.

His whole body started to tingle like needles. He curled his fingers into his hand, but it was all shaking. He brought it up to his mouth, and more pills slipped through his loose grip.

One dropped on his tongue, and he rolled it back into his throat until the pill slid down.

In a near instant, his throat loosened.

He gasped in breath as his hands continued to shake. With the feeling starting to return to his numb fingers, he dug into the ground and clawed up both dirt and pills. He lumbered on his knees over to Kevin, who scratched at his face and throat.

"*Quit,*" Miles gurgled out as he grabbed onto one of Kevin's hands and pushed it away. With the other hand he shoved two pills into his mouth, along with some dirt, and forced Kevin's mouth closed. He rubbed Kevin's throat, and the other man gasped for air.

"Oh-kay," Miles slurred and fell over near Rat, who was face down. He grabbed the thin man on the shoulder and lifted him to his side. Rat's eyes were rolled up in his head, but his mouth hung loose.

Miles dropped a pill on his mouth, but it rolled out and fell to the ground.

Miles squinted hard, forcing his body to work harder. "Work with me, mate," he grunted. He picked up a pill and put it in Rat's mouth again, but it sat there.

"*Fuck,*" Miles hissed and stuck his finger into Rat's mouth, and shoved the pill down his throat.

Rat's eyes refocused and his mouth came down on the finger in his mouth, not with teeth but his lips, sucking it on the way out.

"Eeww, fuck!" Miles near gagged. "I think I'd prefer you had bitten it off!"

Rat didn't hear him, he only rolled and breathed.

Miles looked between the two and was content that they both would live. He grinned and chuckled. "Remember when I said you had to stick these up your ass?" He shook the pill bottle. "Good thing I was joking, right?"

Kevin stared at him before he fell back flat from exhaustion.

THE WHOLE ADVENTURE was turning out to be a woefully long waste of time now that they were empty handed.

Miles wasn't sure, but the footage was likely lost. All the electrical equipment was dead, but he had some small hopes that it had only fried the batteries and not the footage itself. There wasn't a damn thing he could do about it either way.

To make it all the worse, Kevin kept whining.

"It wasn't a *real* nuke." Miles had said as they walked back toward Moscow. "That was a phantom class nuke. They're not the kind that make you grow a hand out of your ass, mate. The Soviets developed it. Smaller scale, tactical explosion with much less radiation, but something akin to an EMP for the human nervous system. You drop that bastard on some—well—on some other bastards, and it cooks all the little shitheads out of the area without making it uninhabitable."

Miles was mostly talking out of his ass again, but at least this time, he had read an article about it a year or so ago.

"I don't *fucking* care! I still can't feel my dick!" Kevin rubbed his crotch.

"Quit being a baby. It all comes back. We got that pill down your throat, didn't we?"

Rat nodded his head in a near blur. "You many times?"

"I what?" Miles glanced between Kevin and Rat.

"You take this medicine many times? This problem? You have that medicine, so you must have taken it many times, yeah?"

"First time, mate. You think I like the taste of nearly suffocating? What'd I tell you before? I'm a boy scout, always be prepared and all that. I have a string of condoms in my bag too. Play your cards right, and I might loan you one." He nudged Rat.

Miles was in a surprisingly good mood all things considered. Nearly dying always did that for him.

"Oh, so it *is* the first time?" Kevin shot him a sharp look. "You *don't know* that I'm going to get feeling back?"

"Come on!" Miles chuckled. "You're *fine*. You got hit with a lot of low dose radiation, but you're *fine*. Your little winker didn't turn cold and die. You had a brush with death and now all your little bits are crawling up into your stomach. *Trust me*. A good night's rest and your diddly will be as good as new."

Miles certainly wasn't sure of that, but what else was there to say? That in theory, everything should be fine, but he wasn't a doctor.

He wasn't much of anything.

Just an asshole.

Oh, here we go again. He felt the smile curdling on his face, so he forced himself to stretch it all the further.

That's what *she* had always said to him.

She'd say it with the most annoying tone of voice he could imagine.

"You're just an asshole."

It was his ex-wife again. He was thinking about her. She always spoiled the mood.

It didn't matter that they were traipsing through the Russian countryside with aliens threatening to bear down on them—or that he'd just survived an explosion—his pain-in-the-ass ex-wife was still living rent free in his mind.

He liked to point a finger right at her and say, *that's where it all went wrong.*

When the show began to fall apart.

When the money started to dry up.

When all the fun in his life went tits up.

"*Shailene*," he spit it out like a curse.

"What?" Kevin asked, momentarily forgetting the numb feeling between his legs.

"Nothing." Miles shook his head. "Just keep moving."

9

JOHN WINTERS WAS one of three living people in all the world who knew what it was like to be president of the United States.

He hated it.

Jeremiah Stanton, the keeper of the *Book of Secrets*, had spoken candidly to him before they started reading.

"This is the loneliest job in the world, Mr. President, and before we begin you have to swear to secrecy what you read within this book. You can't share the secrets with anyone outside this room. Not your children, not your wife. No one."

The world was crumbling around John. The Soviet Union was collapsing, leaders were being assassinated, and his own daughter was God knows where, but once they opened the book...

"Let's begin."

He hadn't been able to stop.

John ended up clearing several hours worth of his schedule to keep reading, going through the words of each past president.

"...nuclear bombs smuggled into L.A..." was a line explaining a declaration of martial law.

". . .Iranian oil reserves aimed to topple the world market. . ." was another passage on Middle East War.

". . .*designed super virus contained in Burma facility. . .*" gave the reasons for the failed cover up of the American coup.

John couldn't say he agreed with each action, but he understood the pressure each president had been under as they held the weight of each decision in hand and judged.

He was under a similar problem.

Launch missiles against the Soviet Union while they're on their knees. And hey, they might even have automation to return fire, but so long as you kill more of them than they do of you, what's the problem?

Tick.

Tick.

Tick.

The doomsday clock, but now it wasn't counting down to Armageddon, it was ticking away the moments John had left to make a decision, a retaliation against the Soviet Union.

But he hadn't been the only person to carry such weight.

Others had, and their stories were in the Book of Secrets, and there was a continuous message.

You're going to do things that no one will understand.

Some will hate you.

Some will love you.

But only we will understand you.

Only we know the price you'll pay.

John was thinking of that price even hours after they'd closed the book and he'd gone to have dinner with Cora.

There were no secrets between him and his wife before.

There would be now.

He dismissed all the staff and he was here alone with her now, but this still wasn't his home. This was the White House, and no matter where he went. . .

The job went with him.

"John, we have to talk about Eli," Cora told him, her hand resting on his elbow.

John barely heard her. It was hard to get his head out of the meetings where they talked about how many lives would be lost in a nuclear exchange.

"Between fifty and a hundred American lives if we act fast and disable their defenses. Two or three times as many for the Soviets if our initial strikes are successful." A general had been talking.

Fifty and a hundred.

The man was talking about millions.

Fifty to a hundred million.

"John," Cora said more forcefully and pulled his arm.

"What?" John said coming out of his daze.

"Just go talk with him." She gestured toward Eli in the living room. He was on the couch watching TV.

John felt bad, he hadn't spoken more than a few sentences to the boy for the last few days. He nodded to Cora and went into the room.

"How you doing buddy?"

Eli's head twisted up toward John. "There are three now. One is hurt, and he is strange. He has a scar. The other two will have to eat him."

John frowned and glanced toward the TV. It was a cartoon of a talking bear bouncing around. "What?"

"They were all going to be kings, but the one with the scar doesn't want to share anymore. He wants to take it all."

"Buddy, what are you—"

"He's going to kill everyone, and then he'll come for me."

———

JOHN SPENT the rest of the night trying to speak with Eli but never really understanding what he was talking about. In the end they watched a little TV together and went to sleep.

John awoke the next morning with the distinct feeling that there was a rope around his neck and he was being dragged.

The first order of business was meeting with his Chief of Staff, McAndrews.

"Mr. President, I have your appointments set out for you, and I sent them to your data pad. But you don't need it, I can just walk you through each of them."

"It's frustrating not knowing what the hell I'm doing until I wake up each morning." John picked up the datapad and opened up the file.

McAndrews fanned out his arms. "Hey, I'm just here to make your life easier. A walking calendar book. You tell me what to do and it's done. As soon as you get your bearings we can adjust things to how you like them done."

John scoffed at that. Would he ever get used to what he was doing? He looked through the list. It was daunting. Appointments and calls with seemingly every corner of the government and several foreign dignitaries with concerns about what was happening in the Soviet Union.

"I don't even know who runs half these damn committees."

"I know who does Mr. President, and if need be, I can take charge for you. Half the damage here is that you don't have all your essential staff. We could wipe half these meetings off the sheet if you got a new Secretary of State, and not to mention a vice president. Do you have anyone in mind."

"I'm thinking about it." In truth, he hadn't been. Who the hell could he even ask?

"Well I booked Tom McIntyre for your first meeting after lunch. Figured you'd want to meet that bastard on a full stomach."

"Why'd you put him on there at all? I'm delegating that one to you," he joked.

McAndrews laughed at that. "I know you two don't see eye to eye, but he's the head of the Senate. Not to mention he's been requesting a meeting since the day after you were sworn in."

"Doesn't take a wolf long after they smell blood."

"Yeah, same for an old dirty bastard in Washington."

John laughed at that. "Yeah sure."

He spent the rest of the day in a near dizzying speed of meetings, but John swallowed his pride and made everyone slow down and explain things to him.

There was no way to be in charge if he didn't know what the hell was going on.

After lunch he went to the Oval Office and kept on working until McIntyre arrived.

The secretary buzzed him in.

Year ago, McIntyre had a collapsed artery in his head. Most thought it would be the death of him, but he was saved by skilled surgeons. They called it a miracle.

John had other words.

They rebuilt synthetic veins that could be seen against his tight paper thin skin. The synthetic veins pulsed in waves like they were breathing.

The end result was that McIntyre lost almost all the feeling in his face, and he often forgot to blink. But when the cameras were rolling, the bastard always seemed to grin, blink and give the appearance of still being anything other than a barely living corpse.

It was only in private that he let that all drip away.

Tom McIntyre entered into the office looking every bit the bastard he was. His face was flat and emotionless, and he looked more like a half melted candle than a man.

When Tom remembered to blink, he always did so slowly as if the whole process was unnecessary, but it was expected of him.

"Good afternoon, Mr. President." McIntyre drew out each word with his strained voice.

A lot of pundits mocked his voice on late night TV. They liked to act like he was some barely functional idiot, but John never bought it.

Tom McIntyre was one of the most dangerous men in Washington.

Few men knew how to turn the gears of the state as well as Tom McIntyre.

"Majority Leader," John greeted him and motioned for a seat.

"Please." McIntyre winced as if his title was painful. "You're the President now, and you're *Mister President* to me, but you can certainly call me Tom."

John cracked a grin and nodded his head. "Well then Tom, not to be short to it, but I'm a busy man. What would you like to discuss?"

McIntyre took the seat and leaned forward, his head half tilted away as he stared at John with his good eye.

Then he blinked.

A long lazy blink.

It happened so slow, that John half felt like reaching over and using his own fingers to speed the process.

"I know these circumstances are peculiar, Mr. President, but I wanted you to know that the Senate is fully behind you. We want to see you empowered and justice for our wounded Democracy."

"I appreciate that."

John couldn't help but think though.

This could have been an email.

"Mr. President, you and I have had our problems."

That was saying it lightly.

They were nominally of the same party, but they had their disagreements.

Serious disagreements.

"But we've got something here." McIntyre held up his hands. "Really have something. Control of the presidency. The Senate. The House." The words drew out, along with the crinkle in his voice. "Opportunities like this are once in a generation."

"Opportunity is a hell of a way to say it. You read the same news I do. War brewing. Congress bickering. Debt piling up. Insurrections blooming. Feels like I'm building a sand castle in a hurricane."

"Americans are never better than when there's disaster afoot. Brings us all together. I'm willing to put all differences aside and work with you on defending America."

John nodded. "We're going to need all hands on deck, Tom."

The vein in his head began to pulse. Maybe he needed a bit more blood in his brain?

Then his face crinkled, seemingly working up to a blink.

Tom went silent as he took a long, five second blink.

"But how's the shoe fit?" A second passed before he spoke. "You were always a foreign affairs expert, but monetary policy was never in your wheelhouse."

"No, but I'm a fast learner."

"You know, you being in charge doesn't mean keeping things the way they are. These are all Warren's men. Him and his *Blue Collar Dream* initiative. You know as well as I do that's all pork with a pretty name. Put lipstick on a pig and it's still a pig."

"What are you driving at, Tom?"

Here was the meat of it, the real purpose of the meeting. John could tell by how the cold bastard leaned in even further. "*Clean house. New policy across the board. I've got names and you've got seats to put asses in—excuse me—put their behinds in.*" He cracked his lips in a wet smile.

John dismissed it with a shake of his head. "You asked me how the shoe fits? Well I'm just tightening the laces. I can't say the policies look to be performing badly, and I have a large agenda at hand. I'm not in a position to dismiss half the staff."

"Half?" Tom raised his eyebrows. "I was talking about the *entire* staff, top to bottom. Frankly, you're no Warren, and the world needs to move on from his cry baby, pencil thin policies. *The Cold War* is hot now. We're on war footing." Tom stared for a long moment, and this time he didn't bother blinking. Instead he leaned back in his seat and crossed one leg over the other.

He was getting comfortable.

Tom went on, "Washington isn't so big that there aren't secrets, and I have more ears at the wall than most." He paused to lick the edges of his dry lips. "You're overwhelmed. Even if you do fill every spot with your own names, the seat might just be too big for you, John. You didn't sign up for this. Everyone knows you were trying to get out of politics." Now he blinked. Long and slow. "No one will blame you for stepping out. It wouldn't be particularly hard either. We've got it worked out, all you need to do is—"

John frowned. It wasn't hard to notice that Tom already dropped *Mr. President* in favor of just *John*.

"You're asking me to resign from office?"

Tom puckered his lips and raised his shoulders. "All I'm asking is for you to do the right thing."

Why not then? John had to consider it. He certainly didn't want to be here, and who would fault him for stepping away and allowing someone else to take the seat?

"And who after me then? You?" John asked.

"Oh, *God* no." This time, when he smiled, John was sure it was the first earnest smile since he entered the office. "I've never had any ambitions beyond Majority Leader, but I have a few names that I know I could work well with."

Something stirred in John, and from any other person on any other day, and he might have considered the offer more carefully. But that smirk on the half dead toad sealed the deal.

There was no way in hell he was letting Tom McIntyre get his fingers into the presidency.

"I'm not leaving the presidency, Tom. Not yet anyway. I'll be running things my way."

The smile faded on McIntyre. "I urge you to reconsider your position. Everyone has secrets, John, and Washington knows yours too."

"It's Mr. President. Not John. And we're done talking." John dismissed McIntyre with a tilt of his head.

Tom grinned again, a dribble of spit rolled down his cheek. Of course he couldn't feel it. His eyes looked painfully dry, and were reddening around the edges, but he couldn't feel those either.

McIntyre chuckled as he got up from his seat. "You say that because you're short sighted. You don't really understand your circumstances. You don't have a *single* loyal man or woman on your staff. Half of them are telling me what's going on, and the other half are telling the opposition party. Warren was bought and sold in so many areas, he had their loyalty. But you, *John*, you were always the lone wolf of the Senate. You don't have a goddamn friend in Washington, only enemies. You think something as silly as a war is going to garner you support?" McIntyre let all the emotion slip off his waxy face. "I'm going to let you think that offer over for a few days. And after that, I'm going to gut you on the Senate floor. I'm going to draw up every dirty secret you have and paint the walls red with your insides. It won't stop with you either, John. Your family is all fair game. Not my rules, just how we play the game in Washington. It's—"

John had heard enough. "Get the hell out before I have you dragged out."

"Well, *Mr. President*, you always did like seeing yourself on the news." McIntyre blinked again, long and slow, and grinned. *"They're going to have a lot to talk about soon."*

10

SOMEHOW, Alice could feel a pulse inside her brain.

The hive mind.

Her skin crawled but she could feel *them* out there in the world, moving beyond where eyes could see.

They could feel her too within the hive mind, and their long wet fingers would reach for her, not in anger, but in curiosity, and she could feel them run through the folds in her mind.

But their touch was wet. And each time she felt it, they left a little more of themselves. . .

And there was a little less of Alice.

How strange.

That's the most that would come from their thoughts, as most had simple minds and did not consider things deeply.

But Alice steered them away.

"Don't take that road." She pointed out to Marat on several occasions, who was looking worse by the hour.

His skin was starting to yellow, and the purple lines of his veins were becoming ever more obvious.

"How could it be happening so quickly?" Moller asked Alice while

Marat ran off to puke on the side of the road. "The Germans live with it."

"They do, but even they get chemical treatments in their food to slow the process. He doesn't have any immunities or defenses." Alice watched him as he threw his head back and heaved once more, throwing everything up. "His body is eating itself."

Alice took the wheel from there, and they passed others in cars, moving in all directions.

Any city or town with a train line was compromised, and it had spread through all of the Soviet Union. Alice could feel their little pockets everywhere, and they would soon consume everything and there would be nowhere else to go, not here.

Soon, there would be no place safe in the Soviet Union.

The cronux would grow and grow until there was nothing left.

And those poor confused bastards moving toward Moscow or somewhere else east?

They're already dead.

They ended up spending a few nights off the road, but Alice could barely sleep.

Even though she was exhausted, she fought it as much as she could, because each time she closed her eyes. . .

She felt like the Archon was going to be there, like an intruder hiding within the dark corner of a bedroom. And if she slept a bit too deeply, his pale powerful body might stride over to her, and wrap his pale fingers around her and pull her deeper in.

Then she would sink down. . .

Down. . .

Down. . .

And she wouldn't be a person anymore.

She would be his.

So she tried to sleep as little as impossible, but instead, took stims. They were just little pills she could swallow when no one else was looking.

The lack of sleep made her half insane, but at least she was still human.

"The road." Marat shook his head and pointed, and even that seemed to be a struggle for him. "Not good."

There was a massive traffic jam ahead of them, cars piled up on either side of the road. Some had pulled into the gutter on the side and got stuck or broke down. Others were sitting right in place, apparently abandoned.

There had been an attack.

That much was obvious with the broken glass and smoldering cars. The car closest to them had the windshield broken in, and now had jagged pieces of glass coated with blood where someone had been pulled out, others were much the same.

Alice could practically see it in her mind's eye, as she glanced toward the woods on the other side of the road.

The cars had been stopped here as the swarm fell upon them. The cronux would have come out from the trees on the distant side, their teeth snapping, and their tentacles jittering.

She imagined the broken, bloody bodies of the once-men, staggering on shattered knees and torn off feet, their jaws loose in an endless howl as they followed side by side with the cronux.

The people in the car would have seen them.

Some would have tried to drive, and maybe a few got away, but most of the cars ended up in the gutter. And there were surely people who abandoned their vehicles to run.

Alice looked toward the woods on the other side.

They wouldn't have made it far.

"We shouldn't stay here, we're going to have to find another way," Moller said as she stared out the windshield.

"No, the swarm isn't here." Alice grabbed her rifle from the back seat and popped open the door. "But something else is."

"*Shit,*" Moller hissed and got out with her rifle too.

"Should I—?" Marat frowned.

"Stay in the car!" Moller barked.

Alice had her eyes dead forward along with the nose of her rifle as she spoke, "They're not far, Moller. That car's out of gas and all the roads might be like this. Let's find one that works and keep going."

"Agreed." Moller came up behind her.

There was only the sound of crunching glass beneath their CAG boots as Alice and Moller walked amongst the rows of vehicles, but the more they looked the further the line was. Alice shook her head. "Better get Marat here. Let's leave the car. I'll keep on ahead."

Moller headed back, and Alice weaved between the cars. Her skin started to prickle and she felt them close by.

There was a tightness in her back, and Alice could imagine the dead parasite inside her body, with its little wisps spread out and curled around her spine.

She could swear she felt them tightening as if it was still alive, a part of her forevermore, while the little frayed ends twisted and scratched inside.

A creature was close, she could feel that too, just as easily as if it were calling to her.

And it was, inside the hive mind.

Here...

It whispered, its call strained and weak.

Here...

She weaved through the broken cars and saw one brown sedan sitting by itself.

Here...

Something was dragging across the window inside, leaving a dark smear across the glass.

I have been forgotten...

Alice approached, staring down the barrel of the rifle. As she got close she could see inside.

Hungry...

A torn body, so ravaged that Alice couldn't make out any features beneath the caked blood. It was missing an arm and a tentacle sprouted from its stomach, and lazily clawed around inside the car.

The body was in the back seat, still belted in and unable to get out.

The sound of Alice's feet on the pavement stirred the creature to life. It raised its gnawed hands and thrust them uselessly in her direction. The tentacle frantically slapped against the inside of the vehicle as its bloody head knocked back and forth on its shoulders.

The diagnostics screen inside Alice's helmet flashed warning colors and gave small readouts of body temperature and the heart rate.

It didn't have one.

No blood was moving inside the creature, no organs were powered.

It was just meat and the parasite's wisps laced throughout, somehow puppeting the entire body.

And Alice could see it.

Not with her eyes, but with the pull of the hive mind, she could feel the parasite, deep inside the body's arm, its little wisps grown deep.

Alice pressed the clasp on her helmet and let it rise up. She took it off and kneeled to set it on the ground.

The creature thrashed and fought with a hungry urgency.

But Alice reached out within the hive mind, and saw the thin red veins from the parasite.

In the real world, she was standing feet away in CAG, with her rifle in hand.

In the hive mind, she moved in blackness, her bare feet touching the cold wet ground, for this was a living place.

The parasite was a raw thing within the hive mind, a half formed being the size of a child, with the face of a demon. It hunched low, and watched her come close, the red veins pulsing as if there were a beating heart.

Had Alice created its form here in the hive mind? Had she given it shape in a shapeless world?

She didn't know, but she was sure this was what it must be like to be a Harbinger.

Alice reached out for the veins, the parasite curled its chin up, its little needle teeth chittering, and she half expected it to snap.

Instead she pinched the veins down and took control.

You are mine.

Alice settled her mind, and in the real world, the creature within the car calmed. Its arms settled and the tentacle eased down.

Alice watched it for a moment, then she brought up her rifle, took aim, and fired a round into where she knew the parasite to be.

The whole body rocked and then sagged.

"Winters!" Moller shouted. She and Marat rushed up between the cars to come up alongside Alice. "What's wrong? What was the gunshot?"

Alice pointed at the dead body in the car. "Just that." She reached down and picked up her helmet and sat it on her head. Her helmet sunk and popped air as it snapped into place. "Let's go find a car and get moving."

IT TOOK the better part of two hours of walking through the pile up before they got to the end. Alice could imagine all the cars careening into the back of each other as the cronux fell upon them.

Marat staggered and needed help. She couldn't imagine he would survive many more days, and the damage he had now may be permanent.

They found an old gray sedan at the end that had been abandoned, and still had three quarters of a tank of gas. The keys were still in the ignition.

They piled in and Alice took the wheel once more. They did pass the occasional car going one direction or another, but they didn't stop. Alice could feel the creatures stirring out in the woods as they passed. But with her mind she gently nudged them away.

Even as they sped down the road, Alice was inside the mind of one. She felt it chewing through the bloody meat of some animal it had killed in the woods. She felt it twist its head toward the road as their car approached.

"Where the hell is everything?" Moller asked.

"They're here," Alice said, and with an easy push, made the creature look away. "They just can't see us."

It took a few hours more of driving before they were close to the propaganda center. They blew through an unmanned checkpoint and headed up toward the station.

The round compound itself was little more than a base for a massive satellite dish angled toward the sky.

"This place." Marat said as sweat dripped down his face. "It is very, uhh." He blinked hard and searched for words. He glanced between Moller and Alice and then gestured with his hands, one above and shook one below.

"Underground?" Moller asked.

He nodded. "It is underground. Very underground."

"You said it was maybe decommissioned?" Alice asked. She pointed at a parking lot. "I think not."

There were rows of cars parked inside.

"Oh no." Marat shook his head. "Maybe soldiers?"

Alice could feel inside the building. It was crawling with creatures.

They'd gotten inside.

11

IT WAS EARLY in the day and the sun was rising. There was still snow clinging to the trees and the landscape of the Russian forest, but the way the sun's rays hit the snow made a beautiful shine.

It also made a glare that blinded people approaching from the other end.

Endo and Dark Ocean were taking advantage of that, as they set up along the road, deep within Soviet territory.

A military convoy approached, so Dark Ocean set up an ambush.

Endo found the dial beneath his chin and rolled it back, magnifying his sight.

A single Soviet tank rumbled forward, with two soldiers ahead on foot in heavy CAG.

Even from this distance, Endo could see the small burning pilot flames at the end of the flame troopers' weapons.

"Dark Ocean, confirm position," Ito's voice rang over the comms.

One by one, each of the six members of Dark Ocean confirmed their positioning.

"Hold," Ito ordered.

The convoy moved at a slow speed, but Endo stayed frozen in place.

The ice and snow on the trees was starting to melt and the water dripped down.

It hit right across Endo's face screen, and he saw the blur of water roll down each time.

Drip.

The two point men walked past and the tank rumbled by.

Drip.

Another bead of water rolled across Endo's helmet screen. He could see it fall and dive down in the air before it hit.

He didn't move.

Several large personnel carriers—essentially trucks with large beds —followed behind the tank.

Drip.

A drop of water rolled down and followed the same vein as the others down his face screen.

A squad of soldiers came up in the rear, twelve in all. They were conscripts, and were lightly armored. Open face helmets and standard body armor.

Drip.

"*Go,*" Ito growled.

Before the last drop of water had hit his screen, Endo burst out of the foliage. He had his rifle in hand and fired three rounds into the squad leader's upper chest just below his chin where there was no armor plating. The man stumbled back, throwing blood across the snow.

There was an explosion to Endo's left as Dark Ocean attacked the tank and the flame troopers.

Endo paid it no mind as he snapped off half a magazine's worth of ammunition into four different men, picking his targets one at a time.

Everything had happened so quickly the enemy was taken by surprise and unable to react.

With so many of their friends already dead, the conscripts gathered their wits and raised their rifles. Endo shot another directly in the face before he could fire a round, but the others let loose on him.

Red flashes of light peppered Endo's screen indicating damage to the armor, but Endo ignored it. The armor could take the hits so long as he was quick, and the enemy imprecise.

Some dodged for cover behind the personnel carriers, while others kept aim at Endo.

Another round shattered off Endo's helmet and made his head rock back.

He was getting sloppy, and it was dangerous.

But why should he care?

The thought occurred to him, even as his body took control of his mind and worked on its own, drawing his uranium split blade from his forearm sheath.

Why shouldn't Endo let the soldiers gun him down now? Wouldn't that be in service to the Emperor? Could he then die and let the suffering end?

Endo was vaguely aware of his knee pressing down on a man's chest as he sunk the tip of his sword into the man's sternum. The man rattled around beneath him.

Endo suffered, and so did this man.

What was the purpose?

Where was the music and the smell of paint?

It had been so long since he could find the memory of his father painting.

His body took control once more as his thoughts drowned him.

Perhaps Endo really had died when he saved the Emperor, and any sensation or memory of the paint since then was but an echo. Perhaps now he was nothing but a revenant, a thing with no real purpose but to kill.

When Endo found himself again, he'd already killed another man. He had the man pinned to a truck with his sword. Endo pulled the blade out, making the man gurgle and collapse to the ground.

Endo swung the sword and the blood splashed across the snow.

This hadn't been hard. These men weren't soldiers. Only boys drafted into service.

But what were boys as far as war was concerned?

All hands hold a rifle.

The fight raged on as Dark Ocean finished killing the soldiers. Endo looked back only long enough to see the Japanese commandos swarm the tank.

That wasn't Endo's mission.

The truck was.

It had come to a halt. Someone in Dark Ocean had killed the driver or blown the engine block.

It didn't matter.

Endo moved toward the back and grabbed the long fabric that draped over the large truck bed.

It might be that he would pull it aside and there would be another squad of soldiers. Perhaps they would be armed with heavy weapons, and a blast from a launcher would end Endo's life.

That too didn't matter.

He jerked the fabric aside and jumped into the back.

Women, children, and men all screamed and cuddled together.

Peasants.

Civilians.

This wasn't a military convoy. It was a refugee escort.

Endo froze in place as one of the babies began to cry and a woman near him begged for his life.

But the sword was still in his hand.

Was this the will of heaven?

THE REFUGEES WERE ROUNDED up and separated in small groups, by age and gender, so that their interrogations would not affect one another.

Several members in Dark Ocean could communicate in Russian, but only Endo spoke it flawlessly.

He was given the task.

"We're going to make a perimeter and scout while we talk to them," Ito had told him as he chewed on a cigar. "You seal them off in groups, and find out what they have to say. Tell them if they comply, we will strip them of their weapons and they will be allowed to leave on foot. Their fate will be their own."

So then, one by one, Endo made his way through the groups, and for several hours he took them away to hear their stories. Something in his stomach began to writhe and squirm like a demon in his gut. It painfully rubbed his insides.

But now wasn't the time to try to subdue the pain. He only ignored it.

He spoke first to an old woman with a sun bleached dress, who had already seen many horrors in her life.

"Monsters. They kill and eat, and the dead rise up again."

And then it was a boy, too young to hold a rifle, but old enough to understand that things would never be the same.

"They took my mother."

Each had a story.

"No eyes, but they had teeth. So many teeth."

Each a scar that would never fade.

"I saw him turn when it got into him. It squeezed so tight there was nothing left. Only the monster. Then he stood again."

Endo knew that the world had changed, that something horrid was now here.

But hadn't it killed the enemy of his people? Was this not the will of Heaven?

Each time he finished his questioning, they all asked him the same.

"What will you do with us?"

And each time, Endo told them what he was told.

"We will take your weapons, and you will be allowed to leave."

It was only when Endo got to the old man, the only adult male in the group, that he was asked a question.

After the old man, who had a long gray beard and a bald head with liver spots, had told Endo his story, he leaned.

"See the girl there?" the old man pointed and Endo looked.

A young girl with a knit scarf and pale blue eyes he could see from even here. She squeezed a ragged doll that was missing one arm.

"She's only eight," the old man whispered, his voice hoarse. "She likes to paint, and ever since she saw them take her brother, she hasn't put down that doll. He gave it to her."

None of that mattered. Why should Endo care if a girl painted or carried a doll?

So why was he looking at her? Why did he feel a strange tension in his neck?

The girl couldn't possibly hear them, but she looked up at Endo. She couldn't see his face, not while in CAG, but he could see hers.

What was she to the world?

Endo looked away.

"Let the children go," the old man whispered, his eyes wide and glasslike.

"You will be allowed to leave. We will take your weapons and—"

The man grabbed Endo's wrist, and though Endo couldn't feel it, he imagined the man's hands were strong from a lifetime of work.

"I know what men do to young girls in war. I've seen it. Do what you want to me, and the others who are old, but please, let the children go."

The man's eyes were wide and wet, but they were also hopeful and pleading.

"Swear it."

Endo did not remember much of his youth before Three Raven. There were only sparks, and even those were questionable, but he had a vague impression of his parents on the last day he saw them.

He remembered the tears.

But those were tears of joy.

This man's tears were of fear.

His synthetic intestines curled and rubbed the walls of his stomach lining. It felt like a demon was clawing him from the inside.

"Swear it," the man said again.

"Yes," Endo said before he considered otherwise. "I swear it."

Something in his voice, even if it was from a face behind a CAG helmet, must have satisfied the old man, as he squeezed his eyes shut, let go of Endo's armor, and nodded his head.

There were others still to be interviewed, but Endo could not forget the man's face.

Or the promise he'd made.

Endo was no fool.

"We'll let them go."

That's what Ito had told him.

But Endo knew what kind of man Ito was, and Endo was not that kind of man.

He'd simply forgotten himself.

Endo pressed the latch on his helmet, and it popped off. He fished a tube of food out of his jacket and bit off the edge then slurped it down.

He needed his focus.

He looked back at the man. "Can you drive the truck?"

The man leaned up, and his eyes grew wide.

"Yes."

"Then go. Quickly."

ITO SAT ON A DOWNED TREE. He had his helmet off and was loudly chewing on a piece of jerky. His cold eyes watched Endo as he approached.

Ito hacked up and spit a glob of snot before he spoke, "What'd they say?"

"They're running from monsters." Endo said, his voice flat.

Ito chewed for a moment more before looking to either side. Both Saito, with his constant malicious grin, and Mori were there. Nakamura, the fifth member of Dark Ocean, was scouting.

"If they were hoping to avoid monsters, it seems they fared poorly," Ito joked.

The other men laughed under their breath.

Ito tore off another piece of jerky. Spit ran down his face as he chewed it. He wiped it away with the back of his hand.

"Elaborate," he ordered.

Endo shook his head. "They don't know. Something happened in Moscow, and it spilled out. It was only a few days ago, but it's spread across the rail systems touching every corner of the Soviet Union."

Mori raised his hands in disbelief. "Then why haven't we seen a damn thing? It's Soviet propaganda. They're losing the war and so they're trying to blame it on something."

Ito swallowed what he'd been chewing. "No. We haven't gotten near any major rail systems. Something happened though. The Soviets caved in far too easily. Without their support, the North Japanese folded. Something bad happened." He pointed his finger at Endo. "But monsters?" He grunted. "I've seen enough horrible things to know that monsters are real, but they're all man made. So whatever that is that's fucking things up." He gestured toward Moscow. "Hopefully it eats their hearts out, and we're here to make sure it happens." Ito stopped and he looked over at the people. "How many women are there?" he wiped the spit off his chin once more.

Endo felt an itch crawling up his back.

But he was loyal.

Obedient.

"Fourteen."

Mori flashed his eyes at Endo. "Any pretty ones?"

Saito laughed

Endo didn't.

"No," Endo replied.

Ito stared at him. Somehow, even beneath the CAG helmet, he knew what Endo was thinking.

"Tell you what, Endo." Ito rose up from his seat and puckered his lips. He gestured with his thumb behind him. "How about you take a two hour walk?"

Endo stepped back and shook his head.

Ito twisted forward and scowled, as if to question Endo with a glance. "My aunt was in a Soviet camp. She went in and never came out. We're not going to do anything to them that they didn't do to us."

The truck started in the distance.

Mori leaned up from the tree too. "You hear that? They're getting in the truck."

Endo could feel the balance of the land start to shift.

But as he breathed. . .

He smelled paint.

"What'd you tell them to do Endo?" Ito demanded.

"I told them to leave."

Ito's eyes sharpened. "Go on a walk Endo. That's an order."

In another life, Endo would have joined the profession of his father.

"*Go. Now*," Ito hissed.

Endo would have been a painter.

Mori and Saito placed their helmets on. The helmets hissed and clicked as they locked into place.

But in this life, Endo was not a painter.

He was an artist of a different kind.

Endo shook his head once more.

"Losing your goddamn mind." Ito snapped up his helmet and placed it on his head. It sank down and locked in place.

Endo kept his pace backward as Ito gestured for the men to circle around.

Each was a deadly warrior with years of combat.

But only Endo was Three Raven.

"What is it you want?" Ito lifted his rifle off the ground and then held his arms out. "You want us to kill you?"

Endo could no longer see Ito's face, but he could tell by the pitch of the man's voice that he was smiling.

"We're not going to kill you Endo." Ito took a step forward and pointed a finger. "Not you. You're too valuable. Too much of an investment." He let the rifle fall loose on its strap and he drew a large blade from his back. He flipped a switch and the pommel stretched far enough that he could fit both hands on it. Not quite a sword, but a short bladed staff.

Endo had seen the man wield it before in deadly fashion.

The others drew their edged weapons.

Ito stopped his prowl forward and stood casually. "Here's what we're going to do. We're going to cut you up, and then we're going to take the pieces back to Japan, Endo, and you know what'll happen? They're going to *scoop* the bad and rotten parts out of you, sew you back up, and put you back into the field, and we're going to keep doing that until there's not enough left of you to sew together anymore. But I'll tell you what." He held up a finger. "One chance. One *last* chance to be a good soldier and do what you're told. Drop the sword, and your helmet, and go sit down."

Endo held his place, and spoke a single word.

"*No.*"

This was the will of Heaven.

LEAVING Leningrad to burn was one of the most painful decisions Garin had ever made, but not the worst.

"I need you and your men to hold the line, Nikitin."

That was the worst.

But his old friend and most loyal officer snapped off a salute.

"It's been an honor, sir."

And with that, Garin left his men to die.

But they weren't the only ones.

On the way to the evacuation ships, he'd seen a great many civilians lined up and pleading as they were shot and their bodies were dropped into the water.

Garin had seen such things before, but he'd never grown jaded to it, and never ordered such things on a casual basis.

But something had gotten into the group before, and it could not be risked again.

Russia could not be risked again.

Berlin was the next sizable secure location within the Soviet Union, and was far enough from the radiation zones of Germany to be safe for those without medical treatment, so they took what civilian vessels were operational and the few remaining military ships and crammed everything in. Whatever was left, be it medical supplies, munitions, or equipment, was destroyed with explosives.

Even in the harbor, as they pulled out, Garin saw the chaos of people swarming the ships. As the crowds waiting to enter panicked, some were shoved into the water and there were gunshots in the air from soldiers trying to hold order.

Garin had lost the city.

He had failed Moscow.

And as his vessel left the harbor, he listened to the comms link of his men as they died.

He'd owed them that much.

Leningrad had been his responsibility—his failure—and it had cost Russia dearly.

The enemy was smart, calculating, and deceptive.

He'd misjudged them.

He would not do so again.

They took the ships further down the sea and sent out scouts for a proper landing zone. They found one in Poland.

Garin split his men into two groups. One group landed in Poland with intentions of liberating nearby cities under siege. The other went ahead to secure Berlin, which was currently under assault.

Berlin had set up military defensive structures, but it still wouldn't last against a sizable army. They'd also cleaned up much of the radiation problems that plagued Germany, but there were some lingering effects that could hinder the troops. Garin decided to lead that mission personally, and gave orders to his troops landing in Poland.

"Your mission is no longer to destroy the enemy or to take land. Your goal is to move in quickly, aid Soviet forces that are in combat, and retrieve any accessible civilians."

But a question came, "*What about those under siege and trapped in their homes?*"

"Leave them."

Decisions had to be made, and there was only so much they could do.

They carefully planned which cities they would aid. There were smaller towns and military depots that were under siege nearby, but there was no time, and Garin's men could only seek to aid those that were in convenient locations, or had sizable assets to obtain. The others would be left to fend for themselves.

So was the way of war.

Garin left the rest of the orders to the men in charge of the rescue force.

His focus was drawn on Berlin.

A scout returned and removed his helmet. He saluted and Garin asked him for a report. "Berlin disabled their rail systems early and threats were contained to an outer perimeter. No sizable force has pierced them, but they are in continual engagement with an assaulting force. The enemy is there in sizable numbers. Berlin themselves estimates the enemy to be at two or three hundred thousand strong."

"*Fuck,*" an officer hissed.

Garin silenced him with a look, and then focused on his communications officer. "Broadcast a signal with Berlin. Tell them to end heavy bombardments, but keep up frontal position firing. We're going to perform a pincer movement."

Everyone had their job and the men fell into position to carry out orders.

Berlin wasn't far from the landing site, so they moved fast.

But in Garin's mind a clock was ticking.

A countdown to when his strength would fade.

They were quickly burning through fuel and supplies. Berlin would have more, but what would they do when that too had been burned up?

Tough decisions would have to be made.

So was the way of war.

Garin's command center was a mobile unit, essentially a large semi truck trailer that parked and folded out.

Garin had to step outside while the trailer was parked and began to unfold with loud metallic clicks and bursts of air. When it was finished, he stepped back inside to see a row of television screens with the feeds of his ground troops.

Garin sat with his staff and waited for the battle to begin.

"Here we go," he whispered.

NAIL KUZMIN WAS ONLY one year into his conscription and he'd already survived one major battle.

The Fall of Leningrad.

He'd been born there. His family was from Leningrad. But when he entered in for his term of service he was sent to the 2nd Guards Red Army under Major General Sergei Garin.

He'd spent most of his time there performing drills and marches in positions where European observers could see him, if only to remind the bastards that the Soviets still had a military that could march.

As a conscript, he wasn't given CAG, but basic armor. He'd been glad for it, as he'd hated the CAG training, especially the part about having to piss directly into the suit.

He wished he had a set of CAG now though.

Kuzmin hadn't any real idea what was happening. Even the average citizen knew that most of the information from the state was bullshit, but Kuzmin saw one of the monsters for himself.

He remembered how terrible it was. A pale white beast rippled with muscles and a mouth like a crocodile's. He remembered watching it open and snake-like tongues jutting out to snag a running man, and then it sucked him in.

Chomp.

Chomp.

Chomp.

That sound had been so loud. Kuzmin could hear the bones break.

He'd fired on the creature, but was pulled away, and for all he knew, it was still out there eating.

General Garin had taken them back to Leningrad, and Kuzmin was elated. He hadn't been able to communicate with his family for some time now, but if Leningrad was safe, then so were they.

When they arrived in Leningrad, Kuzmin called his parents from a service phone, hoping to hear from them or his sister.

No one answered.

General Garin had everyone on round-the-clock duty as they prepared the defenses of Leningrad, but there was the occasional moment to rest.

Kuzmin was able to persuade his sergeant into allowing him to go on a provisions run. He carried out his duties, but then he stopped by his parent's home.

It was empty.

Not ransacked, or disrupted.

Simply no one was home.

Where had they gone? Had they been traveling when things happened? Had they gone to collect his grandmother? Perhaps they were with a neighbor, taking solace in the company of another?

He didn't know.

They just weren't here.

With each passing day, Kuzmin lost more and more hope.

And then the horde fell upon them.

Kuzmin had been one of the lucky ones that made it onto the ship, but as he was leaving, all he could think about was that hope was lost.

His parents? His sister?

They were dead.

Only he remained from his family.

Now amongst the other conscripted soldiers, Kuzmin had changed.

They'd all lost someone, no one still living hadn't, but while the others were afraid, Kuzmin was angry.

He hated them.

His parents were the kindest people he knew in the world. When they saw him off to boot camp, his mother baked him his favorite pastry.

Now they were gone. . .

. . . and he would never know what happened.

When it came time for the engagement at Berlin, Kuzmin volunteered for the front.

After landing, he was crammed into an armored personnel carrier and went on an hours-long drive speeding down some road with only the occasional stops as the convoy cleared the roads.

There was firing and explosions as they engaged small pockets of the enemy as they headed toward Berlin.

The other conscripts clustered around windows and watched.

Not Kuzmin. He had his ass in his seat and eyes down, and took in deep heavy breaths, with the faint smell of piss and sweat in the air.

When the personnel carrier stopped, the armored door on the back fell open, providing a ramp down.

"Go, go, go!" his sergeant screamed and waved his hand out.

Each man got out, and ran, rifle in hand.

Whatever General Garin's grand designs or tactical designs were, it didn't matter.

Kuzmin had gotten what he wanted.

He was right in the vanguard.

Professional soldiers in full CAG fought next to him, firing their rifles at the creatures breaking from the city's front.

In the distance, Kuzmin could see Berlin's massive buildings, but smoke choked the sky, as defensive barriers set out to block the creatures had caught fire.

Kuzmin took aim at a pale beast and fired, whether he hit or not, he had no idea, but blossoms of black blood popped up on the creature's hide.

It turned its massive head toward him. The creature had three jaws in a triangular formation. They popped and opened, drawing lines of spit as it screeched.

The horror of the sight made several of the conscripts stumble back.

Not Kuzmin, he roared back a response.

The creature charged the line, and snapped up one of the CAG soldiers. It whipped its head back and the man went sailing through the air toward the creatures.

Kuzmin fired until his rifle went dry, then he fell to a knee and dug another magazine from his vest.

"Run!" someone behind him screamed, but Kuzmin held his spot

They killed my mother.

He smashed the magazine back in as the faces of his family raced through his head.

They killed my father.

He took aim at it and fired. This time he knew it was his shots blowing apart its neck and exposing the raw meat underneath.

They killed my sister.

More rifle fire blasted it and the creature spun down collapsing to one side, and jittered as others continued to fire into it, ripping its stomach apart.

"*I'll kill them,*" Kuzmin said to no one in particular. He came up along the creature, and its head waved, still barely alive. "I'll kill every one of them!" he roared this time and aimed his rifle, letting go of another blast. The shots cracked against its skull until it broke in and blasted apart its brain.

"I'll kill every fucking one of them!" Kuzmin screamed and ran forward to join in with the charging rifle team.

THE 2ND GUARDS RED ARMY had fought like dogs let off the leash. Garin's men had made him proud.

He'd watched the soldiers under his command obliterate the enemy.

They pinned the horde between Berlin's defenses and Garin's men and cut them to pieces.

"Is that a conscript up there fighting with the regulars?" Garin had asked as he narrowed his eyes on one soldier's feed. "See that he gets a CAG and move him into that squad."

His command unit rolled into Berlin amongst the cheers of soldiers and civilians, but there was no time for honorifics. Garin got out and immediately met with the local command and saw them consolidated into his forces.

They then began improving Berlin's forces with the 2nd Guards Red Army supplemental forces.

This had been a successful engagement, but he was sure the next would be more dangerous.

After Garin had every member of his staff on some vital task, he sat down alone in the Berlin military affairs command center.

Numbers continued to turn and twist in his head.

He considered how many mouths he had to feed. How many tanks and trucks he had to guzzle gas. How many bullets and bombs he had left.

He kept arriving at the same answer.

Not many.

Garin's men had performed well today. They had engaged the enemy. With no concern for their own lives, they threw themselves at the monsters and cut them apart to buy more time.

Now what would he do for those dead patriots?

Surrender.

Not to the monsters, as they surely wouldn't allow such things, but to American and European forces.

As standing Grand Marshal of the Soviet Union, he would surrender so that they all might live.

So that Russia might live.

Garin was a very staunch and serious man.

But sitting in there, contemplating the surrender of the Soviet Union to foreign enemies... He eyed the bottle of Vodka on the desk.

He needed a drink.

He reached over and picked it up along with the glass. He popped the top and poured himself a drink while pressing the comms button on his collar.

"Yes sir?" an officer responded.

"Send in my communications officer." He sat the bottle down and lifted the glass. "We're going to make contact with America."

He took a drink and hit the comms button again.

"Do we still have access to the phantom class missiles?"

"Yes sir."

"And the reports are that they are emitting from a black site bunker just outside of Moscow?"

"Yes sir."

"Then prepare for launch." He downed the last of his drink. "We're going to drop the last of our payload onto that bunker."

THE MEDS HAD DONE something awful to Miles, and now his stomach felt like it was turning inside out.

Maybe it wasn't the meds. Maybe it was the radiation. Maybe your stomach is turning inside out.

He considered that while walking, but came to the only obvious conclusion.

All the more reason to sit down and have a drink.

Inside out stomach or not, the walking had worn him and everyone else out and they agreed to camp out a night before heading into Moscow. There they planned to take a day or two rest, gather supplies, and come up with a new plan, but Miles was certain that Kevin wanted to find a car so they could get to the border, like that would be an easy task in itself.

We're a long way from the border, mate. And the trains are certain death. Gettin' home won't be no walk in the park.

When they had gotten close, they hunkered down as a train went speeding in. Miles hid in the brush and looked up to see that all the windows were busted and something that looked like an inside out gorilla was walking around.

Miles only wished he'd gotten a picture of it.

Rat led them up closer but even he started to get concerned. "I see more of them moving. It is getting dangerous. We need to be very careful. Maybe we gather supplies, sleep, and then leave?"

Miles nodded his head. "You just get me a place to sleep and we'll figure out the rest tomorrow."

They snuck into the city, moving quietly between the overturned vehicles. There were still buildings burning in the distance. It seemed some massive fire was consuming a portion of the city. They even saw a brown truck drive up to them and put the window down. The man was dark skinned with a thick beard. He called out to Rat and the two spoke for a moment before the truck drove off.

"What'd he say?" Kevin asked.

"He told us we should not go. Everyone is dead." Rat frowned and watched the man leave.

It didn't matter. They went in anyway and found a provisions supply store, just on the edge of town. It had already been looted and the front windows were busted, but that made it all the easier to step inside.

Most of the goods were kept behind a plexiglass wall in Soviet stores, but someone had pulled this one's down.

Kevin climbed over and dug out what remained and handed it over.

Miles ripped up the plastic on one of his ration bars and held it up toward Rat's. "Cheers mate."

They clicked the bars together and feasted while guzzling bottled water.

"Tastes like shit," Kevin said between bites, but continued to eat.

Miles nodded in agreement and chewed down three more himself.

When they'd eaten their fill, Rat talked them into letting him go have a look by himself. He was by far the best at moving quietly amongst them, and Miles was in no mood to argue. His feet hurt like hell.

"Have at it." He saw Rat off with a wave.

The city, from what Miles could tell, looked like it had been picked clean and the monsters moved on, still, he was in no mood to have his face eaten.

But he had a nagging feeling in the pit of his stomach.

What would be the point of all this if the footage was wiped? The best he could hope for now was to get somewhere safe and stick his thumb back up his ass while the bills piled up.

Miles groaned and leaned back. He put his hands behind his head and stared up at the ceiling.

Maybe I should have just stuffed the pills down the muzzle of those two and let yourself choke to death, huh? Least then somebody would have thought you were a swell guy. Course, they also would have thought you were an idiot with all those other pills laying around, but they would have said, 'Wow, he died to save us! Bit stupid and all, but he died for us!'. They wouldn't have expected at all that you just died because that was the easy way out. They might have even—

"Who is Shailene?" Kevin asked, interrupting Miles' thoughts.

Miles blinked hard, and he glanced over at Kevin. "Told you. It's nobody."

Kevin glanced over from his seat near the window. "Oh okay."

Miles half growled with irritation and looked back to the ceiling.

Anyway, where were you on those suicidal thoughts?

Before Miles could get a good string of miserable ideas going, Kevin interrupted again. "But who is she?"

"You're not going to leave it alone, are you, you little shit?"

"You want me to?" Kevin glanced his way.

"That's my preference, mate."

Kevin nodded.

A second ticked by.

"She must be important."

"Okay, *okay.*" Miles held up his hands in mock surrender. "She's my ex-wife. Wicked Witch of the West and all that. Bane of my existence. Adversary of a dozen lawsuits. *That's* Shailene."

"Must be some kind of bitch to—"

Miles cut him off with an irritated laugh. "Listen, I might think the word *bitch*, in my brain, might even whisper it from time to time, but I don't call her that and you won't either."

Now it was Kevin's turn to hold his hands up defensibly. "To be fair, I didn't mean it in the disrespectful-to-women way. More to say she was annoying. For example, I'd even go so far as to say you're being a bit of a bitch right now."

"A few hours ago, you were crying about your limp winky stick, and now you're going to take the piss out of me? You're demented."

"I've always been a bit strange. But if I don't talk about something, I'm going to lose my mind."

"Fine, it's a shit story though, mate. Shailene and I got married young before all of *Westwood's Wild World* and all that, but when the money started coming in, she changed."

"How so?"

"You know. Suddenly she's jealous of all the attention I'm getting and how things can't be like they used to be. She helped me build the damn show, but she didn't like how it grew! For God's sake, the money started rolling in, but all she ever seemed to want to do was cry about it."

Kevin wrinkled his nose as if something smelled horrible.

Miles snapped his fingers and pointed. "I know what you're thinking. You think I was *getting a little* on the side, don't you? Had a girlfriend? Dipping my cock in some new apple sauce?"

"New apple sauce? Is that a thing people say? Is that some weird British thing?" Kevin shrugged.

"No!" Miles said a bit too loudly. "I just—my tongue got a little ahead of my brain there."

Kevin motioned for him to quiet down. "Maybe we shouldn't talk about this. You're getting too worked up and there *are* still aliens out there."

"Nothing," Miles hissed. "No other women. I was straight as an arrow! 'Sides the booze and a bit of the. . ." He made a sniffing gesture and rubbed his fingers near his nose. "But that was all to mingle with the executives. You don't meet management without doing a line or two. But, no. I wasn't plowing any fields. But she was *still* bitching."

"I thought we weren't calling her that?"

"No, *no*, I said *bitching*, not that she *was* a bitch. She made it clear to me long ago that calling her the B-word or the C-word was crossing a line. It was a horrible mess for a time, because back in the day I loved to call everyone cunt."

With a slanted grin, Kevin asked, "But you're divorced now? Call her whatever you want."

Miles closed his eyes in painful fashion and shook his head. "You don't get it. You were never married, were you kid?"

"Oh, kid again, we're back to that? And no, I wasn't."

"I respect the woman, I just can't stand her. We had something long ago. The whole shebang with the TV show was something we both worked for. But in the end, she told me to choose, and I did." Miles let out a deflating sigh. "You know what makes it all the worse? I ended up with *this*." He waved a hand around the room. "And meanwhile, she's married and has a kid. Husband's does something stupid. I think he's a programmer or something."

Kevin tisked. *"I'm a programmer."*

"Apparently a shitty one, as we're worlds away from any desk."

Kevin rubbed a hand through his hair. "You know I'm good."

"I know it mate, just bustin' your balls. You've cleverly smashed me to pieces tonight so I just wanted to return the favor."

"No." Kevin's shaggy hair waved as he shook his head. "It's not that. I'm good at what I do, but there was no purpose to doing any of it. Like *why?* What the hell am I any good for if I'm just sitting around the house?"

"Don't be so hard on yourself. You're quite impressive for a scraggly bastard. Hell, we're a stone's throw from demonic aliens, and you're talking with me like it's afternoon tea time. I've been around, mate. Being able to shoot the shit when everything is going to hell isn't no common trait."

Kevin snorted. "I want to actually do something though. I want to help people. But look where we're at. We aren't doing anything here. We just need to go back home."

Miles laughed under his breath. "Mate, you keep going back there."

He pulled down the lid on his off-color eye. "I got my eye torn out for this. You do whatever you want, but I've given up too much to leave empty handed, so I'm not. I'm staying here to get the story out or I'm not leaving. You want to bugger off? Have at it. This is just work for me."

"*Work.* That's right. You're just hoping to get paid."

"Did I ever say otherwise?" Miles gave a flat expression. "Any fool that risks his life for free is just that—a fool."

"So I guess that's me then?"

Miles barely kept the annoyance out of his voice. "Oh, don't go pretending like you weren't counting dollars yourself."

"That was never the point though."

Miles rubbed his fingers together in front of Kevin. "Money is *always* the point."

Kevin huffed and looked away.

Miles waved him off. "Fine, you be that way. Go ahead and work it all out of your system and then tomorrow if you want you can—"

"Do you miss her?" Kevin flashed a stiff look.

Miles felt his guts tighten and his back stiffen. If he had something in hand, he might have thrown it, instead he only squeezed his fist.

"The hell business is it of yours?" Miles fought his lip from tugging into a sneer.

"Just asking." His words were cold, but sharp. And the look on Kevin's face said he knew it.

"Oh fuck off. You know what?" Miles threw out his hand. "Give me my eyeball back. I don't want you carrying the damn thing."

"So you're not going to answer?"

"*Give me my fucking eyeball.*" Miles said through gritted teeth as he got up to his feet.

"Fine, fine. It's not like I want to—"

Miles snatched Kevin's bag off the floor.

"The hell are you doing? You're too rough, you're going to hurt my equipment!" Kevin got to his feet.

"Newsflash, mate," Miles mocked as he unzipped Kevin's bag.

"Your equipment is all fried. That bomb's EMP would have fried all your gear. Little more than a paper weight now."

"Well I don't know why you're smiling then. Would have fried the chips on your eye's cryo then too."

Miles momentarily froze. "The what? That had chips?"

"Of course it did. You thought your eye was just sitting in raw cryo?"

"*Shit*," Miles hissed and went back to digging.

"Here, *here* just give me the damn thing." Kevin fought the bag away and dug out the eye, still snug in a sock.

"Give it." Miles snatched it away and peeled the sock off, and tossed it aside.

He inspected the jar from all angles while his eye floated around in the gel.

"Looks good enough to me?" Miles shot a worried glance at Kevin.

"If my new computer is dead, then so's that eye. It'll just take a—"

A face pressed up against the window and Miles jerked. The jar went loose in his hand. He tried to grab it mid air but instead batted it against the wall. It shattered and glass rained down before the eyeball made a wet slap on the ground. It didn't roll but looked to have flattened on one side.

"Oh—oh." Miles stared at it. He looked at the window once more and it was Rat. He gave them a thumbs up then moved to go around to the entrance.

"Eww, fuck!" Kevin grimaced, looking from the window to the eye. "Geez, I uhh. I'm sorry."

Miles sat back down on his ass and kept staring at the eye.

"Do you want me to—uhh—to clean it up or—uhh—see if there's a bag I can put it in or—uhh—"

"Of course I do." Miles cut a hand through the air.

"So, get a bag?" Kevin took a half step toward the other room.

"No." Miles closed his eyes and violently shook his head. "Of course I miss her. Why do you think I'm such a cunt? I didn't know what I was giving up. But it's her fault too, she could have stuck around, we could have worked on it. Just needed some adjustments.

But no. All I have is the job now." Miles got to his feet again and walked over to the eye, staring down at it. He reached down and found the fleshy optical cord and picked it up." It dangled around his finger as he picked it up.

"Oh *fuck*." Kevin winced hard and looked as if he might gag.

"I saw some of my autographed books sell on online auction for a decent amount."

"Yeah?" Kevin still winced, not liking the implications.

Miles twisted his head to grin at Kevin and jiggled the nerve to make the eye bounce. "How much do you think my eye would go for?"

"God, weren't you all concerned with that eye before?"

"That's me, mate." Miles pulled the eye up level to stare at it. "I roll with the punches."

WHEN RAT SCURRIED into the door, his eyes were distant and shaken. He brought in water, supplies, batteries, and even a few glow sticks. Miles tried the batteries in his cameras, but nothing worked.

"*Fuck*," he hissed as he dug the batteries back out and looked at them. "Suppose my bags are filled with paper weights now. Going to need to find a new camera."

"In Moscow?" Kevin gave him a slanted smile. "You'll have an easier time getting a ticket to the moon than finding a camera."

"Oh really?" Miles said matter-of-factly. "Tickets to the moon just laying around out there you dumb shit?"

"I was being sarcastic. You know the Soviet Union doesn't let just anyone walk around with a camera."

"Don't just let anyone fly to the moon either, mate. We gotta work on your jabs."

"I'm under a little stress here asshole!"

"Just taking the piss, mate, no need to get so sour." Miles grinned and slapped his arm. "Mood's never too dark for a little shit talk."

Rat sat down and glared at the table, not saying a word.

"What's a matter with you?" Miles asked.

"They're still here," Rat said. "I saw them take a man down into the sewers. Not eat. Take. They dragged him away."

Miles skewed his face. "They were playing with him?"

"No. Not playing. Taking. Not hurting. Not biting. Just taking."

"For what?" Kevin asked.

Rat shook his head. "I didn't see. I'm too afraid to look." Rat glanced up and his eyes were glassy and wet. "I saw one of my friends. He always give me his extra food. He was walking with them. His mouth was so wide and his tongue was out, but it was so long. And there were little . . . Little. . . " He looked for the word, but couldn't find it. "*Things* hanging on his tongue. Small little things all over. Moving and shaking as he walked. He's dead. My friend is dead." Rat stared at Miles, as if waiting for a response.

All Miles could do was shake his head.

He was always better at talking shit than he was at consoling anyone.

Rat sighed. "It is getting more dangerous. They are hunting. We must be very careful, very patient when we go outside. They go in and out of buildings. They are looking for us."

"All the more reason to get the fuck out of here then." Kevin said with a tense glance at Miles.

Miles agreed. "Sun's already down. One more night and we make a plan to move on. Where to though is up in the air because we sure as hell aren't taking a train back."

"European Federation border is the only place left." Kevin shrugged.

Rat rubbed the back of his neck.

"Don't worry, mate, you're part of the crew." Miles slapped Rat's arm.

They all agreed to bed down that night, with nothing more but a closed door between them and the outside world.

Rat went to sleep nearly as soon as his head hit the pillow, and Kevin, the bastard, was asleep in only a few minutes.

Miles couldn't sleep.

It was Kevin's fault. His and Shailene's.

She never let him sleep when he started thinking about her.

It'd always start the same way. He'd think about the last time they argued, except this time he didn't have any booze on hand to numb his brain, so he tried to refocus.

"Not doing it. Shit on that," he mumbled toward the sleeping room, half hoping he might wake someone up so he'd have something else to do.

No one did.

"Oh, well isn't that lovely," he continued to mumble. "Could be a creature crawling in here to eat everyone, but why bother when you're tired? Little too much caffeine before bed time and everyone's stirring. Monsters moving around outside, and no one gives a damn."

Still no one stirred.

Of course, they were all exhausted, but Miles had to wonder how it was that those two slept so easily.

Because they're not cunts like you.

There it is. Miles already knew he was, but he had a nice way of just forgetting about it when it was convenient.

Rat, despite being a scraggly thing, took them in when he saw people needing help, and Kevin was only here because he wanted to do something good in the world.

And Miles? He was here for money. He'd said as much hadn't he? At least he was honest about it.

The problem was, without footage, there wasn't going to be any money.

"Fucking Hell."

Miles staggered to his feet. "No use in crying."

He grabbed his pack and pulled it over his shoulder. He thought about it and grabbed a few of the glow sticks too and stuffed them in his pocket.

If he wasn't going to sleep, he might as well be productive.

He crept toward the door, opened it as quietly as he could, and then stepped out into the hallway. Then, with as gentle a touch as possible, he closed it again and made sure the latch caught.

With the door secure, he made his way down the stairs to the streets of Moscow.

He poked his head out and waited a moment until he was confident there were no creatures nearby.

"Here's to all the money in the world."

He took a step out.

ROLES WISHED he had a piece of gum. He liked to chew a few pieces to hide the smell of booze before talking to anyone important.

John Winters had just called him in, and as luck would have it. . .

He was all out of gum.

Ahh hell, why bother? You might be out of a job soon anyway.

That was the word out there right now.

John Winters was cleaning house.

Something had gotten into him, and he started letting loose. Cutting staff.

John Winters should have done it days ago. They were all Warren's men.

Not his.

"He'll see you now." The secretary ushered Roles inside the Oval Office.

The whole place had a presence like Roles was getting ready to attend his own funeral.

Should have worn a nicer suit.

John was sitting behind the desk, his nose deep inside some book. When he looked up, Roles could see the dark circles around his eyes. The president wasn't getting much sleep.

But then again, who was these days?

"Mr. President," Roles said respectfully as he approached.

"Sit." It was a command.

Roles obeyed and didn't say a word. He hadn't been commanded to speak had he?

John folded his hands together on the desk and stared at Roles. John's gaze was deep.

Roles stared back.

When John finally spoke, his voice was darker than Roles had ever heard it. "Did you know that the Soviet command in Berlin made contact with my office?"

Roles betrayed nothing with his expression. "No, sir. I did not." There were few secrets he didn't know.

This was one of them.

"They offered terms of surrender. They're battered. It's a military official in charge now and his force has relocated to Berlin."

"I see." It was all Roles could think to say.

John kept staring, and if anything, Roles was starting to feel the weight of it.

"I called my diplomatic staff and my military officials in for the meeting. I left you out."

"Mmm." An acknowledgement was the best Roles could do.

"What do you think their advice was?"

Oh, Roles had some ideas.

Tell the Soviets to fuck off. Shoot the goddamn Russians in the back. Offer terms of alliance with the cronux to eat the Communist.

Not what he would recommend of course, but he was sure the others had floated those ideas.

Roles left those thoughts to himself. "I suppose they didn't advise a friendly response."

"No. They did not." John took a deep, irritated breath. "I cleared most of the staff then, with more dead wood still to be tossed. Normally I'm an expert judge of character, but I'm in a little over my head all things considered. That said, I haven't particularly liked you."

"I see," Roles said with no hint of emotion. If John Winters expected him to plead for his job, or to be browbeaten, it wasn't going to happen.

"I'm going to keep you around Roles."

That was a bit of a surprise, but Roles kept that to himself. "Yes sir," was all Roles said.

"You're a bastard, but I also think you're a patriot." John took another deep breath and stiffened his back. "And I remember, when they were forming the plan to destroy the Soviet's rail systems, you were one of the few in the room that wasn't salivating. Is that correct?"

Roles took a moment to respond. "No. I wasn't. I have no love for the Soviets, but it didn't seem like a particularly good idea to cut their legs out from under them in the middle of an alien invasion."

"No. It wasn't a good idea." John agreed. "Give me your honest opinion of the current situation. Start with my presidency."

Roles had to stifle a chuckle. "Would you like me to speak freely?"

"Yes."

"You recently had a meeting on tax policy."

"I did."

"What a fucking stupid idea. The Soviet Union is collapsing. The American people are reeling from the death of a president. Washington is in its most bitter stages of partisanship I've ever seen, while much of your staff is debating if we should nuke what remains of the only military between us and an alien invasion. . . And then you take a meeting on tax policy."

"Fair point, and I agree. What you don't know is that Senate Majority leader Tom McIntyre was in here threatening me to either submit to his policies, or step aside. I declined on both accounts."

Roles chuckled. "Ahh, I like him. He knows how to play his cards. Why let a simple thing like the collapse of human civilization get in the way of party politics?"

"Why does it always seem like you enjoy this, Roles?"

"Not everyone gets the job they're born for."

"So you understand the circumstances, and you understand what we're up against? No exaggeration, this entire thing is held together with duct tape and shoe string."

Roles nodded. "You've told me to speak honestly, well here is the truth. I haven't had a very high opinion of you, but if McIntyre gets his way, he'll have a crony in here, and they'll let the Soviets get eaten. We can't have that, so you're the best option."

John frowned. "Appreciate the vote of confidence."

Roles shrugged. "Truth hurts. What are you going to do with the Soviet terms of surrender?"

"The European Federation is discussing if they should allow the Soviets to cross into East Germany. I've got a meeting with the French prime minister, Moshe Sarrazin, after this. I'm going to tell him the United States supports allowing the Soviets in. I think if he puts his weight into it, the European Federation will agree."

"You know those bastards are going to talk until everyone is dead, right? Europeans can't move fast enough. It'll be debates and discussions all the way up until when the cronux are invading."

"Sarrazin is a good friend of mine. I'll see if I can lean on him to speed the process."

Roles grunted. "I'll see what arms I can twist."

John nodded. "Roles. There's also—"

The phone in Roles' pocket began buzzing. He had it blocked for all but important calls. He slid it out of his pocket and looked at it.

This was an important one.

There was a message.

He read it carefully and looked back up at John.

"Sir," Roles said looking up. "I've just been informed. They've found your daughter."

15

ALICE HAD BEEN PREPARED to go into the facility when they arrived but Moller stopped her.

"No," Moller demanded. "You have to sleep first. If you don't, you're liable to collapse in there."

Alice was afraid of sleep.

But Moller was right. She could barely stand.

They agreed to rest until morning.

"How about you? You're not in great shape yourself," Alice asked Moller.

"Better than the two of you. I'll stand guard until morning," Moller said. "If all goes well I'll be sleeping in West Germany soon."

Alice reluctantly agreed and took the passenger's seat while Marat laid in the back and Moller stood watch outside. Alice wondered if she could sleep at all, but it was a moot point. She slipped off the edge the moment she put her head back.

A peaceful darkness came over her like a warm blanket, and it wasn't until she awoke the next morning she realized.

He's not looking for me.

She didn't know why, but the Archon had stopped his focus on her.

It made things easier.

After they got up and ate some protein bars Alice prepared herself and talked with Moller.

"Here," Moller had slapped a communications chip into her hand. *"If you get to the signal booth, jack this into the computer systems. It's a digital flare. It'll signal the rescue team."*

Alice had the chip safely in a belt pocket.

"Sub level two." Marat had groaned and closed his eyes tight. He'd grown much worse over the night. "I try to remember from before. I think the room is there. You have good luck I hope."

Me too.

Alice approached the towering facility alone with her rifle in hand.

The front entrance doors were all cracked open. The metal was peeled back and broken glass crunched beneath Alice's CAG boots as she approached.

"Just be fast," Moller called to her.

That was easier said than done. Moving through the facility, even if it wasn't crawling, could easily take an hour or more. But what if some doors were locked or her access denied?

The halls were coated with yellow paint, which made the blood stains splashed on them all the more obvious.

The facility looked like it had been fully staffed.

She had no idea how many people had worked here but judging by the cars in the parking lot, she imagined fifty or more.

The Soviets liked to keep staff on site for long stretches, so for all Alice knew, there could be even more.

And there were the creatures. So many that the place practically crawled within the hive mind.

She could feel them all in here, and in a way, it was like they all had one little corner of her mind, and were stretching it, making her feel dizzy and light on her feet.

A bead of sweat rolled down her neck despite the suit's environmental systems.

She came to a corner where the hallway split. There was a long bloody streak on the ground that led to an upper torso of a man that had been turned. He was dragging himself around with one arm, a string of intestine trailed behind him. He was headed in the opposite direction of where she was, but her footsteps caught his attention and he twisted his head back and reached toward her with his one good arm. Tentacles slithered out from his insides, but they only slapped and waved on the ground.

She leveled the rifle at him for a moment before thinking better of it and turned the opposite direction.

A light blinked overhead and if not for the yellow walls, Alice felt like she'd stepped back on Mars. Everything was worn down. Even the posters on the wall, all written in Russian with commands and warnings she couldn't read, had multiple holes at the top where they had been pulled off and rehung several times.

All so that the walls could be painted.

That was about all the Soviet Union was good for. The floors were cracked and the posters were old, but at least the walls had a fresh coat of paint.

An ugly yellow paint.

She walked underneath a loudspeaker that buzzed and popped with static as she neared the door to the stair accessway. She used the nose of the rifle to push the door open.

And she saw a monster inside.

She'd been so on edge, that she hadn't been feeling the nudges.

The creature itself was like a massive frog with no head, but two big lips that open up directly from its gut. It held a dead man in its hands and was in the middle of shoveling the body into its mouth when Alice interrupted.

The squeaking door made the creature shift toward Alice. It pulled the headless body out of its mouth and long red strings of spit stretch to the corpse. The fat pale lips pulled back and the creature hissed.

Alice froze in place and raised the rifle, but hesitated.

Instead, she reached out within the hive mind, and pushed it back.

Though it was large and powerful, it was a dumb thing. Its mind was like a thin stick.

Alice simply reached out in the hive mind and snapped it with her fingers.

Its focus and attention softened back to the headless body. It angled its head up and slid the body in whole.

Alice heard the wet slurp as it sucked it down.

She held her breath and moved down the stairs, careful not to disturb the creature as she moved past.

Another bead of sweat ran down her neck and Alice felt light-headed. She tried to focus, but it seemed every time she blinked she waved in and out of the hive mind.

She could see the red veins throughout the facility. When she reached out, it was hard to know if it was with her hand or with her mind.

She was too strung out and tired. She needed more rest, but there wasn't time.

"Get it together," she whispered and snapped her eyes closed for a moment.

When she opened them the world had stopped spinning.

That was good enough.

She had to squeeze her mind like a fist to keep them from stretching too far, but as she got to the door to the next level, she could feel them again.

Once-men.

In her mind's eye they crowded near her, red veins stretching in all directions.

She took two calming breaths and opened the door.

The lights on this level had gone out, but her helmet sensors adjusted immediately. Dim at first, they pulled in ambient light until she could see in dark green tones.

She moved forward within the hollow void of the hive mind, and pushed the veins aside as she walked beneath them, parting the crowd.

So too in the real world.

She stepped out onto the main floor and saw an infected worker. The man had glasses still on his head, but his jaw hung loose and his tongue shook as he moved. His stomach had burst open and tentacles reached out from it, slapping against the wall.

She watched him closely as she moved past. She tensed as a tentacle slapped against her armor and left a streak, but it went on reaching aimlessly.

A woman bumped against her, half shoving Alice against a wall, but that was because she was clumsy from having only one foot. She staggered away, the bone from her shin clicking each time it hit the floor.

There were others with burst tentacles and chewed bodies, all driven by parasites. Alice moved through them. She wasn't a person at all here, not prey.

She was a ghost.

But it was hard to move amongst this many. It took a lot from her, and she was already so very tired.

She could hear her own breathing inside the suit. She was wheezing deeply, like breathing through a straw. She moved away from the crowd and got into another empty hallway.

She rested her hand on the wall and bent over to catch her breath.

Someone screamed in the distance and Alice's hands tightened on the rifle. Someone was dying. She stiffened but looked away.

That wasn't what she was here for.

She tried each of the rooms. Most seemed like small offices, but one had the door frozen in place. She had to kick it in.

The noise brought attention and a cronux came scaling across the ceiling.

She straightened her back and watched it close in. She reached out in the hive mind and brushed it away.

It watched her for a moment, only curious, and then headed off.

With the creature gone, she looked inside, and could tell by the rows of equipment it was the signal broadcasting room.

The computers were still live and running, and the glare hurt her eyes. She adjusted the dial on the light sensors of her helmet, making them dull once more. When it evened out, she pulled out Moller's chip and plugged it into the computer systems.

A few lines of code raced across the screen, but there was nothing else. No indication that it was working.

She just had to trust Moller.

She stepped out of the room and pressed the dial for her helmet to adjust again.

She froze in place. Just down the hallway a man hobbled toward her with his hands up. It was hard to make out too many details with the helmet screen a dark green, but she could see the man had his eyes wide, trying hard to see with only the soft glow of a few indicator lights on the doors and loud speakers.

He whispered to Alice, but it was all in Russian.

She shook her head. "American." Maybe he would think she caused all of this.

"*Help.*" The man must have been in his mid forties. "I see you on screen coming here. *Please help. I need. . .*" He trailed off as he stepped in front of an open door. He looked into the room just as a creature's tentacle slapped around his leg and pulled him down to the floor. The man screamed and reached for her, and his hands caught on the door way.

Alice hurried to him but the creature had already had its teeth in his leg. He cried out with large tears forming in his eyes.

The creature looked up at Alice, momentarily stopping its bite and curled its lips back in a sneer.

She pushed its thoughts away, and raised the rifle.

The man was still looking at her when she leveled it at his head and pulled the trigger.

———

MARAT WAS PROPPED up with his head back flat on the upper pillow in the back seat of their car. He felt like roadkill.

A decomposing rodent.

"*Oh, it hurts,*" he mewed in Russian.

Moller looked at him, but didn't say anything. She didn't speak Russian. She'd gone outside to pace sometime ago.

Marat had lost track of time, but it seemed like Alice had been away for hours and hours, though it might have been only twenty minutes for all he could tell.

Minutes ticked by agonizingly long while his insides constantly threatened to burst.

He wasn't going to survive the night. He knew that much.

This was it. A few more painful moments, and it would all be over.

But did he really deserve better?

So many people had died for him already, and for what?

You might be the only living soul that knows how the gate operates.

He told himself that. He was *too important* to die. The world needed him.

That, or he was just too much of a coward to face reality.

All at once, his stomach jerked and he leaned over to heave out stomach acid all over the seat next to him. He'd gotten past the point of caring about stepping out of the vehicle.

"Shit!" Moller pulled the door open and grabbed his back. Inside her CAG, she could easily pull him out.

He slid out of the seat with little more strength than a toddler as she dragged him to his feet. He doubled over and puked on the ground.

"Just stay with us, Marat. We'll have you back soon."

Marat gave a lazy thumbs up.

He tried to tilt his chin up to smile at Moller, but just as he did, he felt his legs go out.

Then he collapsed onto the ground.

A STRANGE SENSATION rolled over Alice, it clouded out other thoughts.

She was too deep in the hive mind, too lost in their thoughts.

She walked past a scientist, screaming in Russian as several of his former co-workers tore him apart. Either he too had come for her help or they'd dragged him from a hiding spot.

It didn't matter.

There was nothing she could do. Her whole mind and perception was stretched too thin.

It took everything left to stay on her feet, and focus on the hive mind. She didn't try to turn the cronux away or shift their anger. She just reached out within the hive mind and pressed the little red veins away, clearing her path.

She was barely aware. Barely awake.

She was a ghost.

But through that haze, she could still taste the man that was being torn apart. The sensation of his blood igniting the cronux.

One of her eyes twitched. Threatening to close.

She had to stay awake. If she collapsed now, it would all come apart.

And the monsters would see her.

At some point the facility's emergency lights kicked on and now flashed overhead, painting a dark orange glow across her every time it spun, but the light didn't panic her nerves, nor did the *whoop* of the emergency sounds.

She took even, steady breaths inside the CAG to stay calm.

A once-man bumped her as it moved past, knocking her against the wall. Her knees threatened to buckle but she stayed up. She took just a moment to make sure her legs still worked before heading on.

She put her arm out in the real world, and used it to push the creatures aside within the tight hallway, just as she was doing in the hive mind. They shuffled and moved without the barest hint of irritation.

At the end of the hallway, a large, stalking beast blocked the path.

His eyeless face narrowed into a beak that peeled open with three lips parting to display rows of teeth.

He shoveled a corpse into his mouth and swallowed it whole.

Alice ground her teeth and spoke in both worlds, burning more of her strength.

"Move."

The cronux lips sealed closed then he moved from Alice's path.

The lines between worlds hazed. Which one was real? Which one did she belong in?

Alice started to forget.

In one moment, her feet, armored in CAG, crunched on broken glass within the facility.

The next, her feet were bare and in the endless void of the hive mind.

The cronux understood that something was strange here, something that had never happened before. They reacted even though they did not understand.

She felt their presence in the hive mind, shifting about, their wet fingers rubbing across the edges of her mind and leaving residue.

She brushed them aside.

There were survivors here. She heard them scream as they were dug from their hiding places. But was she hearing them in hive mind or the real world? She didn't know.

It didn't matter.

Nothing did.

If they were trapped here, then they were already dead.

How many steps did it take to get to the top level? What path had she taken? Alice barely knew until she stepped from the door of the facility and into the open air.

But was it real?

She didn't know.

Alice staggered and her mind turned over and over, unsure of where she was putting her feet.

Her knees gave out and she collapsed onto the pavement, then she careened forward and her helmet cracked against a concrete curb.

On the ground, her body shook and her eyes fluttered.

She'd gone too deep.

Stayed too long.

The two worlds pressed together, and it squeezed her until she passed out.

ALICE LAY against the cold black floor. Each breath she took was visible in the chill air.

The ground beneath her moved and writhed, for this was a living world.

Alice tried to stand, but she was exhausted and her limbs betrayed her.

In the corner of her vision she saw a pale creature with a fat little body and pointed legs. It hissed and clawed at the ground.

Alice motioned her head toward it and watched the creature inch closer and closer.

"Get away," Alice whispered the words.

The bulbous creature ignored her as it crawled onto her arm. Its tiny little mouth opened and three needle points came out. The tips of the teeth clicked together.

"Get—" Alice started.

It slammed the teeth into her flesh.

ALICE AWOKE SCREAMING. The world spun and moved. Needles were stuck in her arm with tubing flowing out. Men in black full face helmets pawed over her body.

"Get off me! Get off me!" Alice screamed and tried to fight them.

"Winters!" Moller stepped into view. "It's okay! It's okay!"

Alice took several short rapid breaths and looked around. She was in a helicopter and it was speeding in the air. One of the men in black helmets popped the clasp and pulled his helmet off.

"We got your call, we're the pick up team." The man yelled over the noise of the helicopter. "Just lay back and take it easy, we're going to take care of you!"

Alice nodded though her nerves still buzzed.

"Where's Marat?" she asked, but her voice was weak.

"He's here! He's safe!" That was Moller's voice but Alice could barely move her head to see. She was too weak.

The medic leaned forward to look her in the eyes. "We're going to get you back in fighting shape and then we need you on a plane back to Washington in twenty four hours."

"Why?"

"Your father's orders. I'm sorry to have to tell you this way, but you need to know."

Alice felt like she was still dreaming, it was hard to understand what he was saying. "What is it?"

"Your father. He's the president now."

16

As part of his education, Endo had read the classics.

The stories told of honorable samurai, who stood tall in the face of a challenge. They drew their swords and waited for the enemy.

The enemy would draw their blades and close in.

The hero, a man of honor, would stand wait for them.

But this was no story.

This was war.

"Take him," Ito commanded.

Endo did not wait.

He moved against them. Training had long told him that to surprise and overwhelm the enemy was always best.

Mori was a keen warrior. He had facial replacements from damage in combat. His nervous system in his brain was rebuilt with synthetic veins.

He'd been rebuilt once.

Endo's sword went straight through his chin and into his brain.

He would not be rebuilt again.

Saito's blade came down from a high swing, and Endo jerked Mori's body into place. With the strength of the CAG, Mori was little more than a rag doll, and Saito's blade bounced off Mori's back.

"Bastard!" Ito roared over their helmet comms. "Nakamura, Endo's lost his mind. There's a truck coming your way. Head it off."

"No!" Endo swung his sword back and Mori slid off it. When he brought the blade up, it slung blood and brains.

"Come here fucker!" Saito swung his blade and Endo back stepped, watching it soar past his chin.

Ito took a mighty leap forward and swung his bladed staff down. Endo rolled out of the way as the edged weapon slammed into the ground, throwing up dirt.

Both Ito and Saito were warriors. Trained amongst the elite with years of experience.

They fought Endo back, one diving in as the other repositioned with a relentless assault.

With each step back, and each blow deflected, they wore on Endo's strength and sapped his energy.

Yes, both were warriors, but Endo?

He was an artist.

Saito saw that Endo had slowed and moved in, aiming a strike at Endo's midsection.

Endo had planned this.

He leapt into the air, the CAG aiding him beyond human abilities, and swung the blade down across the back of Saito's neck.

Saito stumbled forward and moaned into the comms system.

"Uhhh."

His spine had been cut. It should have killed him.

Instead he writhed on the ground and groaned out his dying breaths as Ito faced Endo alone.

"You were dead!" Ito roared, holding the staff with two hands and facing Endo with a wide stance. "I brought you back! I gave you purpose, you shit!"

Endo leaned up, and when he spoke, his voice was calm.

"You should have let me die."

"Ahh, yes." Ito gripped his blade and pointed it. "I should have."

Endo moved as the blade swung in front of him. He brought his own sword down and took Ito's leg off at the knee.

The man went tumbling down and rolled across the ground.

Still alive.

That was the plan.

Without another thought, Endo turned away and dashed into the forest.

"You're going to leave me here?" Ito screamed at him. *"Like this? You bastard. You fucking—"*

Endo pushed a button on his wrist, and the chat connection with Ito went silent.

He raced through the forest, the CAG giving him long powerful strides.

When Endo came to the truck it was already stopped, and the old man he'd seen was there on his knees.

Nakamura had a gun pointed at him.

"What did you do, Endo?"

"What I had to do."

"Will you kill me too?"

"If I must."

Nakamura laughed, but they both already knew.

Endo could.

"You're a traitor."

"A traitor to some. Not to others." Endo stiffened his back, but kept the uranium split blade in hand. "Ito is still alive, you can—"

"I know. I can hear him. He's promising to kill you. He'll come for you."

"Then you best be fast or he won't have the chance."

Nakamura grunted and aimed his rifle down. "Be seeing you." He took a few more steps before he raced off.

Endo went to the old man. "Get up and back in the truck. Be fast."

The man grabbed Endo's sleeve once more. "There's nothing for us here. But there was a broadcast to go to Berlin. Come with us."

Endo watched for a moment, and he looked up to see the children watching him from the back of the truck. Some were the same age as he when he'd been taken.

He nodded his head.

"Let's go."

17

PETYA ANDREV HAD NEVER MET his father, but he knew his face.

His father's picture was on the wall.

"My boy, my sweet boy. You look so much like him," his mother would tell him.

One look at the picture and that much was clear.

Same jaw. Same eyes.

But that was about all Petya Andrev knew.

Just the picture.

But he also knew how his father died.

"The Americans," his mother would hiss it like it was a curse.

American bastards killed his father.

The precise details were sparse, as they typically were, but Petya did know a little.

His father, a young man at the time with a pregnant wife at home, was serving in Afghanistan when he was killed.

They were told that it was an Afghan, but who had supplied the weapon? Who had offered the training?

Americans.

The Americans killed my father.

Petya had said that as a reminder each and every day of his life.

And each time he said it, a promise was made, both to his mother and his father.

The Americans will pay.

At seventeen he joined the military with his mother's blessing.

At eighteen he was fully trained for CAG and was deployed.

With his rifle and his armor, Petya set foot on the dirt of six foreign nations, and every single Republic within the Soviet Union.

He'd felt the bullets of Belarus insurgents shatter against his armor, witnessed the execution of Ukranian separatist, and enforced work requirements on East German laborers. He'd climbed in rank from a lowly grunt to captain of a special forces team, but he had yet to fulfill his promise.

He'd yet to go up against Americans.

But he waited with patience, and he reminded himself each night.

The Americans killed my father.

He finally got his chance when the American war in Libya began to spiral out of control and the Soviet Union sent his team in.

Supply Libyan Insurgents. Provide tactical advice.

Do not engage the Americans.

Those had been his orders.

He provided the insurgents with weapons and munitions, but it was never for free.

"Tell me where the Americans patrol."

Then, late at night, dressed just like the locals and with the same weapons, Petya set out with several members of his team that all had their own reasons to want to fight.

Even today he could remember sighting down the barrel on an American grunt sucking down a bottle of water.

Petya had waited for the man to tip his head back to drink when he fired.

The man's throat exploded.

There had been an engagement after that, but Petya's team had already faded off and snuck away.

When he returned to his base he got his knife and put a single scratch in the forearm of his CAG gauntlet.

One.

He'd added three more scratches since then.

But with age and rank, the hate inside him began to soften, and he stopped his nightly prayer, and began to focus on the glory of the Soviet Union.

Until Moscow burned.

He saw the reports. Heard the screams of civilians.

The monsters had come up inside the belly of his country and tore it apart.

He didn't know how or why, but he was sure of one thing.

The Americans did this.

The Americans killed your country.

He was a colonel in the Soviet military now with four thousand under his control and serving under Major General Sergei Garin, yet when Stalingrad fell, even Petya had a rifle in hand to fight.

He left Leningrad dragging his deputy through the bloody streets as the buildings burned and toppled. He even watched as the deputy succumbed to his bite and pulled away to attack a group of civilians.

Petya had lost himself then and ran in fear to get to the ship.

Imagine that. A man of his position, with his experience running in fear for his life.

The Americans did this.

The Americans killed your father.

The Americans killed your country.

It would never happen again. He would never turn coward again—despite the odds or the ramifications.

That was his new nightly prayer.

Never again.

So when Major General Sergei Garin (Petya refused to accept him as the assumed rank of Grand Marshal) called the officers in for an announcement and reported, *"We are offering terms of surrender to the Americans so that the Russian people may live on."* Petya knew he had a choice.

Of course, more was said after that. More explanations.

More cowardice.

Petya would never surrender to the Americans. He would never ask his men to give up arms and fall beneath the American bastards.

And he promised himself he would never turn coward and run away from duty.

Never again.

NIGHT HAD FALLEN over Berlin and the sentries suggested no enemy activity.

Petya rounded up a handful of trusted patriots that would be willing to fight for the honor of the Soviet Union and got their weapons.

Of the four thousand men and women beneath Petya, he knew of seven that he was sure could be trusted. Each was an experienced killer, and loyal to the Soviet Union.

All were enemies of the West.

They sat in a quiet room, near Garin's headquarters. They were already suited within the dark red armor of the Soviet Union with the hammer and sickle stamped upon their breast, though their helmets were off and held in hand.

They'd turned off the communication systems within the armor to keep it from being routed to a coordination unit.

This needed to be done quietly.

Petya stood before them. His head shaved and his eyes dark. The room was dark, but the glow of the helmets painted each with a soft light. He turned up the illumination on his helmet.

It was important that each soldier see his face.

"You all know why we're here." Petya's voice was low, and rough. "Major General Garin staged a coup on the Soviet Union and declared himself Grand Marshal."

He paused to look at each man for any sign of reluctance.

There was none.

"Garin is a traitor. He now wants to surrender to the West. He seized power only to betray us. What do you patriots say to surrender?"

"Fuck America," a man with dark blue eyes said.

"The West killed Moscow. Now they want to eat our corpse," a woman with a shaved head said.

One by one they each spoke.

"No surrender."

Each affirmed their loyalty.

"Death before betrayal."

Each proved themselves a true patriot.

"My life for the cause."

Petya took up his helmet and placed it on his head. It sank down and locked in place with a puff of air as it sealed. The yellow camera lenses grew brighter as he drew up his rifle.

"For the Motherland."

SERGEI GARIN STOOD over a table with several of his officers, both soldiers he had known for sometime and others who had joined in with his call from Leningrad.

They acquired a teacher's lounge within the school and turned on the dim light overhead. Several of the officers smoked cigarettes and drank either coffee or liquor.

But not Garin. He was stone sober. His mind was sharp.

He was the one that had agreed to the terms of surrender offered by the European Federation.

But he wasn't sure who would remain loyal after.

His deputy stood before them all, reading from a datapad.

"The European Federation is considering the terms of. . ." The man hesitated before speaking. "Of our surrender. But here are the conditions upon which they will agree."

As each person in the room listened to the deputy, Garin turned to watch their faces.

He'd already read the terms. He knew what they were. With one master stroke, the West hoped to roll back a hundred years of Soviet gains.

But his officers hadn't heard them. And some of them had family that died for those gains. The deputy read the terms, but Garin wasn't listening.

"...establish formal ties with East Germany..."

Garin only watched their reactions.

"...reinstate the Seoul arms agreement..."

An artillery captain curled his lip and smashed his cigarette into an ashtray.

"...disavow ties to Sudanese mineral enrichment sites..."

The chief armor officer closed her eyes and leaned her head back in apparent disgust.

"...immediately end support of Hudaniten rebels in Venezuela... "

One man scoffed and shook his head. Another stared blankly at a table.

"...end claims to Indonesian—"

"Enough." Gavin held his hand up as he rose from his seat.

All the eyes of the room turned on him, and at that moment Garin didn't know if they would agree to the terms, or cut him into pieces.

Garin steadied his voice "You all know the circumstances we are in. Unknown creatures have collapsed Moscow. There is no word from General Secretary Durak Suka-Blyat, and the Kremlin has been confirmed to have been destroyed." As Garin spoke, he took the time to look each soldier in the eyes. "Most of you were with me when we lost Leningrad. The enemy stormed us and cut our lines to pieces and ate us from the inside. Our detailed reports say that we have a mere one hundred thousand military personnel with reports of more soon arriving. We have an unconfirmed number of civilians with more arriving by the day to be set up in isolation until we discover what exactly happened in Leningrad. We all have brothers and sisters out there still fighting. There are still some forces in the distant East, but they too are trapped.

"We are the only sizable force still standing within the Soviet Union, and if we fall then all of Russia will fall. All of our history, and all of our people will cease to exist. Under this deal the European Federation and the Americans will begin offering us support and aid, along with several other agreed upon conditions." He gestured toward the datapad the deputy was reading. "Those things and those places are not our people. They are not our culture. We are. We have a duty to survive because we are all that's left of Russia. If we survive, our people survive, our language, and our history survive. If we act as fools now, there will not be a Russia tomorrow." Garin quieted and waited for the room to speak.

The artillery captain cleared his throat. "Fuck the Hudaniten. A bunch of useless assholes anyway."

A woman spoke, "I served in Sudan. Too hot to bother with even with the CAG."

Others spoke in agreement and Garin nodded. "Then we'll continue our defense of Berlin, and as we regather our strength, we'll press to the center and reclaim the Motherland."

"I promise you all." He looked each of them in the eyes once more. "Russia will live on."

ONE OF PETYA'S men leveled his weapon and pulled the trigger. With a few soft *pops* from his silenced rifle, three CAG killer rounds slammed into a sentry's head. The man fell onto his knees and put his hands up to his head, trying to feel the hole. Apparently two of the rounds hadn't gone through. Petya couldn't see but expected one had only torn through the man's jaw or some other less than lethal place. They moved up quickly underneath the shadows of Berlin and fired more rounds into the man's chest, finishing him off.

The seven patriots formed up along the entryway of the school, and each nodded their head to confirm their positioning.

They waited for Petya's command.

"Go."

The first squared up in front of the door and with a powerful armored kick, the door crashed in. They flowed in with rifles up.

There were soldiers inside, but some had their helmets off or their weapons down.

Petya's soldiers took advantage of the chaos and fired right away, many of them died before they got their weapons in hand.

Petya aimed at an unarmored man reaching for his rifle and put two rounds directly into the man's chest, blowing blood and bone apart.

Another went diving behind a table and Petya fired the CAG killers directly through the cover. There was a loud slap as the man's body fell over.

They mowed the men down as they made their way in.

"This is necessary," Petya had told them before they went in. *"We won't kill anymore than is needed. We have too few soldiers left, but those that die today bleed for the cause of the Motherland."*

They kicked down another door and a man rushed at them. One of Petya's men blew his head off with a short burst.

"We'll eliminate the traitors and all the officers who follow him."

Shots peppered one of Petya's patriots, a young man named Alek. One of the rounds got through Alek's armor and he fell back dead. Petya roared in anger and armed a grenade. He tossed it at the attackers. The explosion silenced them and wood scattered across Petya.

"We'll place in our officers. Good, loyal patriots that love Russia."

They stormed past the smoking bodies and made their way to the teacher's lounge where Garin had set up.

"And I promise you all."

They lined up along the door and prepared to enter.

"Russia will live on."

Again, they waited for Petya's call.

"Go."

THEY ALL HEARD the shouting and firing, but none of the officers were in CAG.

Someone looked at him and asked, "Americans?"

Garin shook his head.

He knew the sound of an AVM-208 when he heard it.

Garin knew who it was.

Petya Andrev had notably not been in attendance.

There was screaming and roaring around the room as men overturned tables and pulled their sidearms. Everyone scrambled for cover and weapons.

Not Garin. He stood his ground.

He would not die cowering.

He folded his hands behind his back and kept his chin up.

The enemy had picked his moment well. They had waited until the staff was stretched thin with duties, and all the commanding officers were in a single room.

Petya Andrev would be the death of Russia.

The door burst open, and Garin watched as the splinters from the wood rained past. Soldiers poured through the entryway, and those in the room fired at them with pistols, but they were near useless against CAG.

A pistol round ricocheted off a CAG soldier and smashed into the artillery captain, blowing apart his knee, making the man collapse and scream in pain. One of the CAG soldiers finished him off with a blast of rifle fire.

A woman grabbed Garin's arm and tried to pull him behind the cover of a table, as if that could save any of them. They fired rounds into her chest, and her body collapsed to the floor.

Another of Garin's men had hid against the wall. He leapt forward and shoved his pistol right into the chin of a CAG soldier and fired, the rounds went through and bounced around inside the helmet killing the man. One of Petya's men grabbed the shooter and threw him against a wall hard enough it might have broken his back, then they raked him with rifle fire painting the wall red.

There was shouting and screaming, blasts of pistol and rifle, but through it all Garin stood in place and waited for the bullet that would catch him.

None did.

A man stepped forward and held up his rifle. "Cease fire!" his voice amplified to a near deafening shout by his helmet. "Cease fire!" It was impossible to tell who it was with the CAG helmet altering his voice, but Garin was sure.

Petya.

A man who'd served with Garin for nearly a decade came up from cover and fired at Petya. A bullet bounced off Petya's helmet.

A useless gesture.

Petya's men turned on the shooter and cut him down.

"Such a waste. . . " Garin said pitifully as he watched the man die.

"Anyone else?" Petya asked. "Hands up and weapons down!"

Garin looked across the room.

Four were still alive. Seven dead.

Garin growled but he didn't speak.

"Take them out of here." Petya pointed. "See if any of them are still loyal to the Motherland."

The four remaining soldiers grabbed Garin's officers and dragged them out. Garin didn't look at them.

He kept his eyes focused on Petya.

When they were alone, Petya pressed the release on his helmet and pulled it off.

He was a deathly serious man with dark eyes and an intense stare.

"Major General Sergei Garin. You are being relieved of command. You will come with me and make an announcement on all communication lines that I have taken control of—"

Garin returned his own stare, and when he spoke, it silenced Petya. "The West will not negotiate with you. They will not begin dealing with a man who seized control in a coup."

Petya took a step closer so he could look down at Garin. In the CAG he was inches taller. "They won't negotiate with me at all. The West surely did this, and there will be no peace for their crimes. Only blood."

"Then you are a fool, comrade, and you've killed us all."

Petya slapped Garin across the chin, and with the CAG, the blow toppled him to the floor.

Garin's vision blurred as he pawed around on the floor, fighting to stay conscious. He tried to speak, but was sure that his jaw was shattered. He lifted a hand up to his face and found several bloody teeth stuck to his chin.

Petya grabbed him around the throat and lifted him into the air with a single hand, still holding the rifle with his other. Garin groaned as his destroyed jaw pressed against Petya's grip.

"You *will* come and announce my command. You *will—*"

"*Mah fuhk'n jowl.*" Garin gurgled blood as he spoke.

Petya tossed him across the room and Garin slammed into a table. Several ribs snapped. He curled his legs in from the pain as he lay on the floor.

"You're a traitor, Garin. A bastard of the Motherland," Petya said as he prowled forward, his CAG boots heavy with each step. "Only a dog would be so cowardly to sell his country to the West. If you won't do the honorable thing then should I shoot you like a dog?" He aimed his weapon, but Garin looked away and squeezed tighter into a ball. A humiliating way for a man of his stature to die.

"Fuhk. Yew," Garin growled.

"Maybe I'll just squeeze your throat until it pops? Traitor's deserve no better." Petya reached down and grabbed Garin by the throat once more.

But he hadn't seen the shard of wood from the broken table in Garin's hand.

With an agonized grunt from his burning ribs, Garin shoved the shard through Petya's chin and up into his head.

Petya dropped his rifle and stumbled back.

It hurt to move so fast, but Garin snatched the rifle from the floor and went to his feet.

Petya grabbed the edge of the shard and drew it out of his face, the splinters dragging out pieces of flesh and veins with it. With wide, fearful eyes he stared at Garin.

But there was nothing to be said.

Garin pulled the trigger once and the rifle kicked hard enough that it felt like it would tear his arm off, and sent new pain burning through his body. It was designed to be fired with CAG armor control. It hurt to use the weapon.

But the bullet did worse to Petya. His head rocked back and he collapsed.

Garin stumbled over to Petya's helmet and picked it off the floor. He pressed a button on Petya's armor connecting it to the comms system.

"Hehn," he hissed trying to form words but finding it near impossible. He reached up and though it hurt he squeezed his jaw together as he spoke. "Fhailed Coup. Neehd shouldiers."

Petya's other men were still down the hall.

The next word he spoke was clear.

"Fast."

MILES STEPPED out onto the streets of Moscow and the world was quiet. But like a fading pulse, there were still small flashes of electricity from lights that flickered on and off.

Say what you want about the commies, but their electrical systems can take a beating.

Miles was sure of that as he saw another train speed overhead.

He walked out into the cool air and pulled his jacket up higher on his neck.

"What the hell are you even looking for?" Miles mumbled to himself.

No camera. No recorder. No computer.

What was the point?

He should have turned around and made a go at sleeping again instead of walking down the streets of an infested city.

But here he was walking beneath the dying street lights.

That was Miles.

He knew that if he got eaten, then tomorrow Kevin and Rat would wake up and have no idea what happened to him. They might even go out looking.

He shot a glance back at the building they were in.

One more go at sleeping?

No. He had a feeling there was something out here worth seeing, and until then he was going to—

Something growled in the distance and Miles dropped low and jolted for the corner of a set of concrete stairs that led up to the rail system. He pushed his back flat against the stairs and waited a few heart beats before looking around the corner.

He didn't see anything at first so he had to squint, but his eyes popped wide.

Something was crouched low and moving from car to car. Miles wrapped his fingers around the edge of the stairs and leaned out further.

He hadn't heard a growl at all, he'd only imagined that.

It wasn't a monster. It was a person. They must have just made a noise while moving.

The person was grabbing something off the ground and looking things over before setting them aside.

Miles licked his lips and considered just heading off on his own way, but for reasons he wasn't entirely sure of, he stayed and watched.

The person had a hood on, but pulled it back as they looked closer at the items he was picking off the ground. It was a boy. A teenager maybe. He looked like he was reading the labels. Maybe he was looking for food?

No. That's not food. That's medicine.

Miles could see it now. The boy was out in front of a pharmacy. Someone had ransacked it and either dropped or abandoned a lot of the meds in front of the store.

Just go. It's no business of yours. What the hell are you going to do for the kid?

Another train came speeding overhead, far faster than it should be. It rattled the rails above Miles and made all the lights shake and blink out. Miles looked away again and pressed his back to the wall and waited for his eyes to adjust to the darkness.

But the lights overhead continued to buzz with electricity and after the train passed, they flicked back on.

Miles took one step in the other direction, but something nagged him.

That same odd instinct.

It told him to look again.

He leaned out over the corner once more.

The breath caught in his throat.

A massive creature was standing out in the distance, around a building where the boy couldn't see. It had two massive legs and no arms. A walking mouth.

The massive mouth opened and spoke with an unnerving, human voice.

"Help me." The words were in Russian, but Miles knew the meaning.

The creature's whole body shook as if to mock crying. It took slow, careful steps forward, its head turning in each direction.

"Help me."

The boy couldn't see it.

Miles clenched his teeth and whispered, *"Don't you move. . . Don't you fucking move."*

The boy couldn't hear him of course. He wasn't even aware that Miles was here.

"Help me."

The boy leaned up and inched toward the edge of the building to look past.

"Don't do it kid," Miles whispered again.

The creature turned its head to either side. As far as Miles could tell, it also wasn't aware of the boy.

The kid inched up to the line.

It was impossible from this distance, but Miles imagined he could see the spit strung between the creature's jaws and its tongue working, twisting into odd angles to mock human words. He imagined the horrible smell of sweat it had as its body pounded forward.

And he imagined the boy screaming, the medicine still in his hand, as the creature chewed his bones into pulp.

"Hey you fucking cunt!"

What the hell just happened?

"You look like a rat turd with legs!"

Miles was screaming at it.

And he'd only just realized.

The creature froze in place, it too was stunned at Miles gall.

You and me both, mate.

That was the last thought he had before the creature bolted in his direction.

"Shit!" Miles yelled and rounded the corner. He shot a look either way and saw more of the same. Broken cars, poorly lit streets, and half collapsed buildings. All with a nice flat street for the creature to run him down on.

Up it is?

Miles bounded up the concrete stairs, his lungs already working over time.

He was half way up when he glanced down and saw the creature step into view. Its large mouth flared open and it tried to step onto the stairs with its massive feet.

It took one awkward step and then another before it fell over.

Its three toed feet were too large for the narrow stairs.

Miles slowed down as he got to the top, and frowned as he watched it.

The creature rolled over and tried again before stumbling and hitting the stair wall.

"*You big bitch. . .*" Miles chuckled under his breath.

The creature screeched again and tried a third time, it fell onto its back and rolled down.

"You dumb asshole!" Miles laughed and grabbed his crotch. "You stupid shits can burn Moscow to the ground, but you can't climb stairs!" He held his stomach and laughed.

Enraged, it roared again and bent down on its legs preparing to lunge.

"*Oh shit.*" Miles took a half step back.

The creature leapt into the air, collided with the stairs a quarter of the way up, but as it tried to stand it ended up rolling back down again looking utterly ridiculous. It huffed with each thump of the stairs.

"*Bwah!*" Miles bent over on his knees and pointed, laughing so much it hurt. "You dumb fucker! You stupid rat turd!"

The creature clawed up to its feet again and even as Miles kept laughing it held one of its feet in the air. Its toes flexed up and down. Then they cracked and flexed low on its feet.

Miles' laughter trailed off as it stepped onto that foot like a ballerina. It held the other foot up and the toes flexed and cracked too, giving it small points to step on.

It then stepped up onto the stairs.

Then the next.

And the next stair after that.

Miles was sure he'd watched for far too long at this point.

"Well hell," he looked either way at the top of the station. Off in the distance he saw another train approaching.

Miles glanced down the stairs and the creature was half way up now. It opened its mouth wide and giggled with a human voice, akin to a small girl.

"Terrifying." Miles mumbled. "Absolutely. Terrifying."

There was a trashcan nearby. Miles yanked it over and rolled it down the steps. Trash spilled out as it tumbled toward the creature but it opened its mouth wide. The can went inside and it smashed down shredding the metal then spit it out to the side.

Miles glanced down the rail to see the train was closing in at an intense speed. He ran toward the edge and jumped down into the pit. He looked back and saw the creature's head poke up at the top of the stairs.

Miles huffed as he climbed over the rails, careful not to touch any as they were electrified. He got to the other side and grabbed the edge to pull up. With a groan, he dug his fingers into the groves of the concrete floor and pulled.

The angle was so awkward that it was hard to climb, but adrenaline powered his muscles and he threw one leg over and crawled the rest of the way. Laying on his ass, he looked to see the creature come all the way up.

Then there was the train. Miles pulled his legs out of the train path moments before it sped in. It stopped in place and a damaged synthetic voice gave commands in Russian while voices screamed on board.

Miles dully climbed to his feet, his eyes wide as he looked up and down the train. There were hundreds of body parts poking out of a living sludge that ran the length of the train. Barely visible heads had their mouths open and screamed. Some of the sludge opened too like a mouth and screamed. It all roared in some painful unity for seemingly no purpose.

Nothing there even bothered to look at Miles.

After a moment Miles glanced through the windows of the train to see the other side. The creature was there.

As the doors on the opposite side of Miles opened, the sludge inside the train screamed even louder. Miles had to hold his ears as the sound was painful.

The creature that had been chasing him had no problem. It focused on Miles and stepped onto the train. Its toes unfolded to a flat foot again and it walked through the sludge, stepping directly onto a screaming face.

The creature roared and smashed its face at the wall and window between it and Miles.

Then the train doors closed and the synthetic, malfunctioning voice spoke again. The train started a slow crawl, taking the creature inside with it.

Miles watched the train move away. The creature, clearly confused now, started running the length of the train to try and stay in position with Miles, but the train picked up speed and it was gone.

As the screaming faded, Miles stood there in disbelief, watching the train head into the night.

A quiet second passed beneath the faltering train station lights. Miles looked to his left and then to his right.

"Well." He still had the sound of the sludge screaming in his ears. "That was awfully strange."

FEW THINGS RATTLED MILES, but a pile of screaming sludge with human faces seemed to be one of them.

He was having a hard time imagining the purpose of it all.

I can understand the walking mouth speaking a human voice. That makes sense. But what the hell was the value of a screaming sludge beast?

Miles was having that conversation in his head as he walked down the stairs, ever careful to watch for dark corners.

A shadow just beyond the stairs moved and Miles froze in place.

The boy stepped forward, the hood over his head once more. He spoke a few words in Russian, but Miles was too flustered to catch any of it.

"Not from here, mate." He patted his chest. "Only English."

The boy scowled with concern and watched Miles closely.

Miles plastered on a smile and motioned that he was going to leave.

The boy held out his hand with a pill bottle. "Mother medicine."

"That right?" Miles nodded. "She close? Your home close?"

The boy listened intently then pointed to a nearby building.

"Back to mother then." Miles gestured toward the house. "Be safe."

"Thank you," the boy said.

Miles felt something twist in his chest, an utterly strange sensation. It seemed to flow out of the boy's desperate eyes.

"No worries, mate," he said nervously and gestured toward the city. "Fuck all this, right?"

The boy frowned, maybe he didn't understand.

Miles smiled and gave a thumbs up.

The boy smiled back and returned the gesture.

Miles grinned again and waved the boy off. He went on his way back to the building.

Miles had a strange sensation rolling over him. He buzzed like there was electricity in his veins.

He felt good. Great even. Not at all like a piece of shit, which was the norm for him.

Didn't even get a picture!

Somehow that thought made him even happier, and he felt like he could sleep easy now.

He was still careful when heading back. He stopped by an abandoned car and waited for a moment, listening carefully for any threat.

He heard some people talking and leaned up from the car. A small group of survivors were moving from car to car. A man with a beard caught sight of Miles and pointed. Several others glanced up over the hood at him. Miles froze in place.

A few painful seconds passed before he waved.

The man with the beard held still for a bit longer and then he too waved and gestured for his group to move on.

The man stood watch as several of his group members moved past. A woman brought up their rear and she was cuddling a baby. The man nodded at Miles and followed behind. They disappeared around a corner.

Miles watched them leave and looked around the city.

Large looming buildings, massive rail systems, countless stores and housing—Moscow had been the jewel of the Soviet Union, but now?

It's all dead. Just crawling with fleas.

He'd been aware of it all before, but it was as if he'd only really felt the suffering of it now.

These people were struggling to get by, and Miles?

He was hoping to film it all.

"You're just an asshole."

That was Shailene's voice again.

Oh great, are we going to start doing this right now? I was in such a good mood.

He tried to stuff the thought as he peeked around the edge of a building and then dashed across a street.

Why should he be torturing himself? Honestly, what was wrong with filming anything here? It didn't make anyone's suffering any *worse*, did it?

If anything it just—

Miles stopped that thought flat.

He saw an old naked man dragging a body down the middle of the street. Miles squatted low behind a destroyed tank and peeked over the edge.

The old man had shaggy gray hair, but walked hunched over as he dragged the body with one hand.

But there wasn't anything between his legs. Just a flat spot as bald as his head.

Miles' jaw dropped open as the old man stopped, chewed something in his mouth and glanced around.

Miles stayed perfectly still and fought the urge to duck lower.

The man turned back and bent down to the body.

Even from this distance, Miles could hear the sound of bones breaking and flesh tearing. The old man came up again with something bloody in his hands. He stuffed it into his mouth, getting blood all over his chin and grabbed the body once more. He dragged it to a sewer hole, and with one hand fit his fingers into the manhole cover and lifted it aside.

The lid banged as it crashed into the ground. The old man dragged the body over and dumped it down the hole, and without another glance, turned around and walked back into the night, leaving Miles to stare at his wrinkled ass.

When Miles was sure the man was gone, he rounded the tank and took a cautious approach toward the sewer. There was no cover in the center of the road, and he stopped to look around, feeling intensely vulnerable, but nothing moved or came after him.

His hairs stood up on the back of his neck as he inched toward the hole. After one last look around to make sure he wasn't being watched, he peeked into the sewer.

It was too dark to see anything.

"Fuck," Miles hissed under his breath.

Before he could think better of it, he fished a glow stick out of his pocket, cracked it, and tossed it down. The glow flashed off until it smacked the body laying in the water.

Nothing else happened.

"Why in the hell would he do that?" Miles mumbled as he stayed just over the sewer entrance.

Why the hell do they have sludge beasts on trains? No reason at all. They're insane and horrifying. There doesn't need to be a reason.

That was the thought rolling around in his head, but Miles didn't believe it. There was purpose to it all for some reason, there had to be. Miles might be a con artist, but he knew from the years on his show that *everything* had a reason.

He turned over and put his foot on the ladder.

What the hell are you doing?

He asked himself that because he honestly wasn't sure.

He went down a few steps and grabbed onto the metal with his hands.

No really, what the hell are you doing?

Miles climbed all the way down until he was practically on top of the body. The stench was horrible, but there was a rock ledge he could step on that prevented him from going directly into the sewage. He strained to see anything with the glow of the light, but there was total darkness a few feet out. He cracked another glow stick and threw it down one side. It skidded along the concrete edge and rolled to a stop. Miles didn't see anything except more tunnel. He pulled out another glow stick and cracked it. He tossed it down the other way, but it didn't skid.

It smacked right into a large fleshy egg not far away. Long, pointed legs attached to the base of the egg stretched in Miles' direction and snapped down suddenly.

Miles fought the urge to cuss but stumbled back. He grabbed the hand railing to keep from slipping on the wet ledge.

The leg punctured the body and slid it closer as tentacles slid out of the base of the egg and pierced into the coming meat.

Panic almost made Miles surge up the ladder but instead he held his place.

Nothing happened.

He took a breath.

Still nothing happened.

Really pushing your luck here, mate.

The egg looked wet with flexible, transparent skin and open flaps at the top. Miles could see something moving around inside it.

Miles slid out another glow stick and cracked it.

Here's hoping I still got my aim.

He tossed the glow stick over to the egg and it fell right into the flaps. It sank down into the gel and Miles could see the outline of what looked like a baby in the womb curled up.

That's what that old man is.

He's one of these things grown in an egg.

There was a loud crack, like tree bark splintering somewhere behind the egg.

Miles squinted and then he dug out another glow stick—his last. He cracked it and tossed it over the egg.

It pegged the slime covered head of something crawling out of an egg.

"Oh shit." Miles hissed.

The hatchling had long hair and large naked breasts. With one hand, she reached up and wiped the slop from her eyes, and then they popped open and focused on Miles.

She opened her mouth and puked up slime. Then she mumbled words in Russian. Miles didn't understand anything, his mind was reeling.

She slithered out her other arm and cracked the edges of the egg to pull her hips up.

Within the soft green light of the glow stick, Miles saw she had nothing between her legs, only a fleshy blank spot.

She pulled her leg out and twisted her head down to look, then back up at Miles. She got free and slipped over the edge of the concrete and down into the sludge of the sewer.

Oddly Miles had instincts that made him take a half step forward to help her out, but he held back. Her head came up out of the sludge and she moaned as she made her way closer to him, sifting through the sewer waste. Still feet away, she bore her teeth and reached for him.

Miles finally refocused.

"Yeah, *no*," he said with a shake of his head.

He grabbed onto the ladder and hurried up it, glancing back only in time to see her reach the concrete ledge.

Miles pulled his legs from the sewer, half afraid she might be reaching for his ankle.

"Shit on all this," he said as he backed away. It was a struggle to keep from sprinting back, but after he got a good distance away before he bent over to breathe and refocused.

They're growing people.

This wasn't going to stop in the Soviet Union. This was going to spread all over the world.

He needed to get back with Kevin and get as far away from here as possible. He could deal with the bills later.

But then there was a question, and oddly he imagined it in Shailene's voice.

"Are you just an asshole?"

Miles thought of the boy with medication for his mother. He thought of the woman carrying a baby and the man that looked after her.

And he thought of the woman crawling out of the egg.

We've got to tell someone. They have to know there's still people here. Not soldiers, but people.

He wondered what that meant. Where the hell could he even go?

European Federation.

He had to go West. No point in trying to go back the way he'd come, it was too far and the trains were down. They had to head to the border and find a way in. . .

And let everyone know what the hell is happening here.

With that thought in mind, he crept back. He stopped between streets and was careful with how he moved. He had to freeze in place for a few long minutes as something with dozens of legs crawled across some high building wall.

Miles heard people screaming in the distance, and he made a silent prayer that it hadn't been the group he'd seen but some other unfortunates.

When he finally made his way back and opened the door Kevin was already up. He gave Miles a relieved look before pointing a finger.

"Where the hell have you been?" Kevin asked. "We were going to go out and look for you!"

"Sorry, I was. . . out." Miles fought back a yawn. God, he could take a nap now. "Couldn't sleep. Won't do it again."

"Where?" Rat asked.

Miles shook his head. "The streets." He narrowed his head and steadied his voice. "Rat, did you know they're growing people?"

Rat frowned as if he didn't understand.

"Growing people?" Kevin asked.

Miles nodded.

"No joke, mate. Big, nasty eggs. Old men with beer bellies, large breasted women, and presumably everything in between. The whole package."

"So what do you want to do?"

"Tell the whole world what we saw in Moscow. That's what we do right?" He grinned at Kevin. *"Where the shadows are deepest, the secrets are darkest."*

———

THEY BID farewell to Moscow and spent the next few days traveling West on foot after failing to find a car they could start.

Miles' high minded ideals were starting to fade with each passing hour.

He had a rash forming between his legs and he'd practically dug a hole through his pants scratching at it. "Hell with this. We need to get a ride. I say we risk it with the next group that passes?" Miles said and the others agreed.

They were on the road for another few hours before they saw a line of two military grade trucks approach, but civilians seemed to be driving them. "Hey, we're in luck!" Miles said to the others and waved his hand.

The truck pulled over and Miles and Kevin plopped down on their asses while Rat talked with the driver.

"Think this'll be like a movie?" Kevin asked.

Miles yawned. "How do you mean?"

"Hitchhikers get tortured, murdered, and eaten, though not in that particular order."

"You know? My balls have been screaming at me for the last two hours, so I'm willing to roll the dice."

Kevin sighed but nodded his head. "I just hope its the murder *before* the eating."

"We've been lucky enough so far. I'm sure it'll hold out long enough to get them to murder us before eating."

Rat was still talking, he pointed back at Kevin and Miles. They smiled and waved at the driver.

"Seriously though?" Kevin asked. "With everything that's going on, they might not be too kind to a pair of Westerners."

"Hmmm." Miles narrowed his eyes and considered. "You know what?" He stretched his legs out and groaned. "I'm still gonna roll the dice. I'm curious how they got those trucks though, mate. Those are military. Maybe they have some weapons—though I do have shit for aim."

Rat smiled and nodded his head at the man then approached Miles and Kevin with a thumbs up. "We go with them! But you must talk to—"

A truck door opened and a man in black armored CAG stepped out.

"*Holy shit,*" Kevin whispered and moved up to his feet.

Miles on the other hand wasn't standing up just yet. If they planned to shoot him, he was at least going to be comfortable. Though he did watch the man curiously. Miles was by no means an expert, but it didn't look at all like Soviet CAG. If he wasn't mistaken. . .

That's Japanese.

The man popped the clasp on his helmet and pulled it off. It was a handsome Japanese man with his facial hair growing a little rougher than usual on account of being out in the field Miles assumed.

"You can come with us," the man said in perfect English. "But you must give me your weapons." He held out his hand.

"We're in luck then, mate, because we don't have a damn thing." Miles sighed, he supposed if they weren't going to shoot him and eat him, then he should get on his feet after all.

"I apologize, but I must search your bag," the Japanese man said with a calm tone.

"No apology needed, I wouldn't trust a man that travels with this scraggly bastard either." He thumbed toward Kevin.

"I suppose you're *funny.*" The Japanese man's tone was flat.

"I make the attempt here and there." Miles shrugged and handed his bag over.

The man carefully went through the bag. When he was content he handed it back and reached for Kevin's. When he was done with all of them he motioned to follow.

"So, mate, got a name?"

The Japanese man glanced back at them. "Kota Endo." And placed his helmet back onto his head. It sank down and sealed. "You'll be safe with us." His voice boomed from the CAG speakers now. He climbed back into the truck.

Miles leaned over and whispered to Kevin.

"What a hard ass."

19

THE ARCHON WAS god of this world. The ground he tread upon was holy. The cronux bowed to him, both in awe and fear.

Worm was not a god.

He was a monster.

He was carried through the gate and up into the land. And was given a single command by the Archon.

"Wait."

Worm was not keen on the tactics of war, but the Archon was. He understood that all things and time had a place.

Worm only waited for his.

"Go."

That was the command now. It came from Janissary who now led the army.

Worm flowed through the darkness, his head careening and cutting as his body pulsed and shivered to sift the land.

His body was fat and wrinkled, but long and flexible.

Worm was not a complicated beast. He understood little of the world, or even his position within it, but it didn't matter.

He didn't need to understand so long as he did what he was told.

He felt movement in the darkness, it came from above. Worm simply moved in that direction, and when he got close. . .

He stopped and waited.

———

ALYONA RUBBED her nose and wiped the string of snot on her pants leg. Her nose had been runny since arriving in Berlin. Supposedly the radiation wasn't as bad here as it was in the rest of Germany, but she had been feeling shitty since the moment she arrived.

She wanted to get chem treatments, but everything was being rationed. The doctor assured her she would be fine though.

She didn't trust the doctor.

She didn't trust anyone.

She heard shooting a few nights ago, down where Garin and his officers had set up camp, but the next morning they assured everyone that it was just a weapon misfiring.

"Like hell." She scoffed, but what was she supposed to do about it?

Just more lies.

Everyone played their own game, and she would be no different. When the officials came around and told them that all civilians would be given work, she volunteered for guard duty.

It wasn't because she wanted to do any fighting, she just wanted to have a gun.

She had one now. Some rifle that she didn't know the name of—not the same thing they gave to the regular soldiers, those had a kick that could tear an unarmored shooter's arm off. She'd never served in the military herself, but she'd shot rifles before.

It felt good to have a weapon in her hands.

She walked the streets with another girl, part of the internal patrols while the regular military went about whatever it was they were doing.

"We're all going to die here, I'm sure of it." That was Alyona's friend, though Alyona didn't know her name. She'd asked twice before, but kept forgetting. She didn't bother asking a third time, there was too much to think of to bother with anyone's name. She knew enough about the girl. Both were refugees, and neither knew anyone else. And still, strangely, Alyona couldn't remember her name.

"Likely," Alyona agreed.

The other girl was nice enough, but Alyona didn't trust her. She didn't trust anyone.

"The boy I'm fucking told me they plan to cut rations again. What's that say about the deal with the Americans? Why are they cutting our rations if the Americans are supposed to give us more food then?" the girl said.

"Whatever they said, whatever you heard, it's a lie. It's all lies." Alyona shook her head, but squinted at a man who was walking oddly. She gripped her rifle and tensed. The other girl did the same. The man put his hand on the wall and threw up.

Drunk.

They both grinned and looked away.

People weren't supposed to be drinking now, but Alyona didn't care. If anything, she wanted to go ask him where he got the booze.

"It can't *all* be lies," the other girl said. "Just most of it."

No, it's certainly—" Alyona trailed off as she felt light headed and started to wobble.

No. That's not my head. The ground is shaking.

"What is that?" the other girl finished.

The ground burst open.

A massive worm burst up through the ground and Alyona fell back. Half dazed she crawled around before she could turn over to look at what happened.

The worm was erected into the air, it's large fleshy mouth opened wide with pointed teeth sticking out.

Alyona's friend was inside.

The girl screamed and swung around like she was on fire. She sagged to one side of the creature's mouth and reached a hand out to Alyona for help.

Alyona only aimed the rifle and fired. Her bullets thudded into with no apparent concern.

The girl screamed more as the worm's body pulsed as if to swallow and sucked her inside. She kept screaming long after she disappeared.

The worm bent down, not bothering to even stop Alyona as she fired another round at it. It made gagging noises, and Alyona expected her friend to be thrown up.

Instead a thing akin to a cat's hairball puked up. Then another. And another. And a dozen more.

It was only when they started unfolding into wet beings the size of children that Alyona remembered her radio.

She was supposed to call anything odd in, but as the small wet goblin-like creatures displayed their teeth, she ran.

A blind, fearful run before one of the creatures smacked into her back, knocking her to the ground. It bit into her arm and tore flesh off. She screamed, and surely others would have heard? Surely someone was going to help?

They rolled her over and she got to watch as they dragged her back to the worm.

She saw the inside of its mouth. A massive, round hole with countless teeth. It widened for her, and she could see the bottomless pit of its throat.

She should have called it in or at least helped her friend.

She supposed she shouldn't have been trusted.

———

THE PATRIOTS that attacked Garin had turned out to be more cowardly than anything else. As soon as their leader was dead, the few others surrendered. Garin would have had them executed, but that would have only brought more attention to the situation. Instead he had them put into cells where they could rot.

It was unfortunate that they hadn't killed him, at least then Berlin could have been someone else's problem. Instead he was left with a shattered jaw and no end to the work piling up.

"We can perform surgery and save your jaw. But you'll have to be medicated for a while and it'll take weeks to heal," the doctor told him.

Garin motioned for a piece of paper and pencil, and a subordinate hurried it over.

He took the pen and scribbled.

No.

He pointed at a man's mechanized limb, then he pointed at his jaw. The doctor nodded.

He still needed surgery, but Garin insisted on localized anesthesia rather than be put out. He was awake and listening as the saw buzzed through his jaw bone.

It was certainly odd the moment he felt the weight drop off.

Fortunately, Berlin had some of the best doctors in all of the Soviet Union, and they worked wonders.

Garin had a fresh jaw with black synthetic skin attached to his nerve endings in no time at all. Nearly as good as his old one though it strangely made his voice raspy.

The next day he was up on his feet again and giving orders, and the first thing he did was send a message to the French Prime Minister Sarrazin agreeing to the terms in exchange for immediate aid.

He waited for their response.

Politicians seemed to work at a snail's pace.

Garin was in his office reviewing a datapad of the replacements that had assumed the positions of the senior staff that had died when a man threw his door open.

"Sir! They're inside!"

WORM SIFTED through the ground until he found a spot that called to him. He burst up through it, and opened his mouth. It was painful to spit up the small creatures inside, but they were tucked into fleshy sacs near his jaws. The muscles in his body contorted and surged to make the sacs pop open.

He spit them all out, and they came to life screaming and attacking those nearby.

Worm's body heaved again and he shot out a thick layer of phlegm that hit a building. It sizzled and burned where it landed. He whipped back and forth, throwing it all into the air with no real concern where it fell.

People screamed and ran, some even fired at him, but he had no eyes to see them, and no real concern for their weapons.

He sank back into the ground and surged up some of the burning phlegm to his lips, it helped to tunnel through the ground. His body shivered and quaked and he surged forward some distance and erupted up into the middle of a room. He spewed the phlegm and it must have hit someone as they screamed even louder than most. Worm fell flat and crushed a person beneath him. Worm's body was sensitive and he could feel the person squirming. He curled up from the ground, leaving the flattened body. Worm twisted around to get his tongue in position and licked the flattened person inside his mouth.

It quivered and shook all the way down.

He liked it when they did that.

He sank into the ground again and started forward. He went further this time before churning up to the surface and came up underneath a tank. He felt its treads turn and they rubbed against his flesh, tearing holes in him. With his nose, he pushed it over and it fell upside down. Worm bellowed and wiggled up from the ground more to careen his head into the tank's underbelly. The burning phlegm helped him weaken the metal and he chewed through the rest.

Several operators were inside and they crawled back on their asses screaming as his mouth closed in on them.

Worm struggled to get in deeper, but he was too fat and the metal hole was too small. Instead he leaned up with the tank on his head and the men rolled around inside it. He thrashed and shook them until they fell into his mouth. He chewed them apart.

One operator hung onto something and waved back and forth as Worm shook it.

With some irritation, Worm gave up. With a groan, he spewed phlegm into the tank, burning the man alive.

A blast smashed into his side and Worm sagged from the pain. He shook the destroyed tank off his head just as a second tank was firing upon him.

Another shell blasted into him and his guts poured out.

He sank down into the dirt before a third shot could be fired, then moments later erupted underneath the other tank, toppling it.

Perhaps they'd thought they'd killed him, but he was not so fragile.

His guts would grow back.

THE JANISSARY HAD BEEN ENTRUSTED with a sacred duty by the Archon, god of this world.

"Kill them all."

He intended to do just that.

While the Archon was a force of power and strength, using his armies to roll over the enemies, the Janissary was not.

Unlike his brothers, he was a thing of finesse.

He did not join the battle lines, but stayed some distance away in a nearby forest, but he could see all, for in this world he had many eyes.

Battles were living things. They shifted and moved. It was not a struggle but a dance.

The Janissary understood this.

Smaller than others, but a keene observer to the art of war, he knew that positioning and timing were important.

He allowed the men to think they were safe.

Then he sent Worm.

Even as that beast was creating havoc, making men afraid of the ground they walked upon, he called forward his second wave.

With a single open hand he gestured toward the city, and all the birds took flight.

Any that would be afraid of the ground would soon be afraid of what flew in the air.

Now he waited with his ground troops.

Timing was everything.

ALL IT TOOK WAS ONE. Garin knew that. One domino to tumble and everything would collapse.

The birds could do that.

He'd gotten the reports of some horrid worm sifting around in the dirt and half expected the ground to erupt beneath his feet when another threat came in of a dark wave moving in.

Birds.

But he was prepared.

"Flame troopers on the roof! Aerials incoming!" he'd ordered.

He set his helmet for video feed and flipped through to see what his soldiers were viewing from the points of conflict. He watched a flame trooper storm to the top of a building and let loose a blast of fire that melted a wave of birds.

They pelted the ground in meat.

Such stupid things, they seemed attracted to the flame soldiers and made them all the more easy to deal with.

But all it took was one.

One domino to fall, one to tumble.

And Berlin would collapse.

"Focus on the birds!" he ordered. "Cook the bastards, don't let them spread the parasites." He reached over and grabbed his comm system operator by the collar. "Put a message to US command, you tell those bastards we're under assault and out of time. They need to send us help or we're dead and this is all *their* fucking problem."

TIMOTHY HAD BEEN at the pantry when the city sirens came on, indicating an assault. He was hustled with a crowd into a nearby building to lock down until the conflict was over.

But Annita, his girlfriend, was back in the workers' barracks.

He could get to her if he moved quickly. He was sure of it.

The civilian managers were busy locking the doors when Timothy found a window. It opened inwardly and was hard to crawl out, but he managed.

The streets were bare when he stepped out, and the sirens had even stopped.

It would be a short run to the barracks, he only needed to be fast.

He took off quickly.

He made it only a few feet.

Something small smacked into his side and he felt an edge stab him.

It was a bird.

Another came and pecked at him.

Then a third, and a fourth, and soon there were too many.

They pecked him all over, and then all at once, burst off him and flew away.

Timothy saw the blood all over his arms, and the little bulbous parasites he'd been warned about.

He felt their little wisps dig into his skin, and he felt the agonizing pain as they slipped into his skin.

He writhed on the ground, arching his back and rolling around on the asphalt.

There wasn't time to think about what he *should* have done. What little of Timothy that was left didn't think at all.

He stood now, a new beast with a new purpose.

He looked back to the window he'd just crawled through.

20

MARAT WOULD SURVIVE. The German doctors were well versed with his kind of radiation sickness.

"He'll need to have his lungs replaced," the doctors told Alice.

"Do it," she ordered.

Marat would spend the next few days recovering, but Alice was having problems of her own. The doctor ticked off a list of medical conditions.

"You're dehydrated, exhausted and your pulse is off the charts. If you don't take a break, you're going to have a heart attack. Not to mention you're having highly abnormal brain patterns."

She spent the first day in a wheelchair because they insisted, but refused the next day.

"You want me to keep rolling around here, then you're going to have to break my knees."

They'd wanted to put her on a flight immediately, presidential orders, but she refused that too.

"I'm not going anywhere."

No one could understand, but Alice could feel something in the hive mind. It was like looking out from a beach and watching the waves crash against the land, and in the distance seeing a tsunami coming.

There were distant pin pricks all coming together and forming clumps.

The cronux were gathering, and Berlin was all that stood in the way between them and the European Federation.

Sitting in her room with a wide window that beat with the poison rain of West Germany, Alice worked on her mechanized limb. She had the synthetic skin on her replacement hand lifted open, displaying the small muscular gears working inside. She wasn't much for fine tool manipulation, but she learned to work on her own replacement limb. She was adjusting the settings because the fingers started misfiring when she got back.

The doctor said it was a possible neural problem from all her strange brain activity.

Alice decided it just needed to be adjusted.

"You're just one person, Winters," Moller said, sitting across from her. "If you head back to Washington we can find something for you to do."

Alice looked up, and wiped away a strain of loose hair. "Do you really think that? That I'm *just* one person?"

Moller shook her head. "You know I don't. I saw what you can do. But your father is the president now and things are different."

Alice looked away and finished with the tool. She pulled it out of her forearm and folded the flaps down. "Something's about to happen, and when it does. . ." The black synthetic skin sealed together, though the seam was obvious. She held the hand up and flexed it open and closed.

". . . I'll be ready."

MOLLER HAD ONLY LEFT Alice a short time ago to head down to check on Marat. He was still out, but the surgery had succeeded. Now he just had a brand new scar down the center of his chest and new lungs. The doctor had told her it was essential.

"Essentially the lining within his lungs is melting and he's drowning from it."

Marat had looked awful, but she didn't know he was *that* awful. Somehow he'd been able to put on a good face.

She didn't know what was going to happen to him after he woke up. The CIA might come and collect him to hear every little secret he had about the Soviet Union and their research.

Watching him sleep, she felt bad about that.

She hoped she at least got a chance to say goodbye.

A voice boomed over the comms system. *"This is not a test. This is not a test. Report to your station. This is not a test."*

Moller wasn't sure what was happening, but she found an official who could tell her.

"The Soviets asked for our help. The Chancellor told us to scramble jets now, but we're on standby."

"What are you waiting for?" Moller asked.

"The Americans."

Moller rushed through the facility, moving past men and women scrambling to get into position and war footing. Many of them had trained for years to fight the Soviet Union, and now they were being called to its aid.

She ran up to Alice's room and hit the door open button.

It flashed locked.

She beat her hand against it. "Winters, open the door!"

Nothing.

"Dammit."

Moller pulled out her comms and pressed the call for Alice. "Winters, you there?"

Nothing.

Where is she?

Moller considered for a moment before it all clicked.

She took off in a dead run to the airfield the Americans used.

Massive American aircraft, both jets and carriers were being prepared for takeoff. Moller ran past them into the hangar bay.

She saw Alice in the distance arguing with someone.

It was a dropship captain, and as Moller closed in she could hear him.

"Sorry, but there's no way." The captain shook his head. "Even if they launch jets, they're not going to send ground troops. I haven't heard a damn thing."

"What's going on?" Moller asked.

"It's happening *now, Moller.*" Alice said. "I need a ride into Berlin."

"I can't give you a ride. You're not certified for drops, and your CAG isn't equipped for them either. You'd fall like a rock."

"I served with the Marines," Alice shot back at him. "I've done drops before, I know what I'm doing."

"Listen, you could have everything you want, but if they don't give me clearance, I don't fly. Orders are to stay grounded. I'm sorry." He shook his head.

"If we get clearance though, you'll take us in?" Moller asked.

The captain made a skeptical look at her. "They tell me you're clear to drop, then we'll go, but this boat has been just for show." He slapped the side of it. "We don't even have a full drop team."

Moller pointed at him. "You finish prepping, we'll be right back."

As they walked off Alice asked, "How the hell are you going to get clearance?"

"Your father." Moller shot her a look.

"I can't just call him on the phone anymore, Moller, it isn't that easy."

"No, but I can get a message to him."

THEY'D GOTTEN the call and immediately moved to the situation room. Roles was one of the few people sitting around the table with John Winters. Rows of screens were displayed in front of them.

Roles' secure phone buzzed.

Few had the number.

He slid it out and read the message.

It was from Moller.

He slid it back into his pocket and folded his hands in front of him on the table.

"*Hmmm.*" He considered things while looking at the screen, seeing images of mapping along with readouts of military preparedness.

John Winters was currently discussing air force capabilities with a general when Roles finally decided to sit up. A few glanced at him as he walked around the table.

"You need to take a shit or something?" A general scowled at him.

Roles ignored the comment as he approached John.

"A moment," he said in a soft voice.

John glanced at the screens and then over to the air force general. "Can you continue your report on combat readiness?" The general agreed and John headed over toward a corner of the room while a few others.

"Not the best of timing, Roles," John said.

"I suppose not." Roles gave a flat look. "It's about your daughter."

MOLLER WAS HELPING Alice fit her CAG on and lock it all in place when the call came through. It was from the dropship captain.

"*Don't know what you did but I've been given clearance. Now if you want to drop with a CAG that isn't equipped for function, that's on you.*"

Alice pressed the call button. "Just get me to Berlin, I'll do the rest."

21

WHEN ALICE WALKED onto the dropship, it gave an odd, dull sound as she went to the bench.

She'd never been alone in one before. She didn't know what a single pair of boots on the ground sounded like.

Moller, fully equipped in CAG, came up behind her and took a seat.

"You ready, Winters?" Moller asked, the voice coming over the internal comm system of the armor.

"I hope so." Alice locked the belts around her and pressed a button on her helmet opening the line to the pilot. "We're clear."

"*Confirmed,*" the captain responded.

She closed her eyes and tried to find her center as the ship lifted up and took off.

With a buzz, the drop cage descended over her, and locked her shoulders down into place while the whole aircraft shook from the flight.

The captain buzzed over again, "*Drop one, we're looking at a twenty five minute flight. Berlin is practically in spitting distance.*"

Alice kept her eyes closed and took long deep breaths. She felt a fog start to roll over her.

A being within the hive mind that felt her coming close.

Janissary.

His touch was not cold or wet, but warm and delicate. He greeted her like a friend.

She pushed him away.

She wouldn't spend her final moments before the drop thinking of the monsters, not when it had been so long since she'd seen her son.

Eli.

She thought of his warm smile and imagined the grin on his face when he found a bug in the yard and held it up to her.

Last summer, there was a night when he woke up screaming. He told her that monsters were chasing him in his dreams. He said he screamed and screamed but mommy wasn't there.

She told him that was only a nightmare, that she'd never leave him behind.

His mother didn't run from monsters.

She killed them.

Even from some distance she started to feel the scratch of the hive mind. It grew inside her brain like cancer.

The parasites were in the city. A small outbreak.

But soon they would grow.

They would eat Berlin.

Alice pressed commands and opened up a grid map of Berlin on her screen.

She knew where the infection was.

"Drop one, we're clearing the zone," the captain said. *"Going to find you a sweet spot."*

"East city block two seventy," Alice said over the comms.

"Say again, drop one?"

"I said target the east city block two seventy. I'm no good a mile out in an open field."

"Negative. Hazard zone. If I miss, you're liable to bounce off a building, drop one."

"Then don't miss."

"You want the risk, it's your call. You game, drop two?"

Moller buzzed into the line, *"Do it."*

"Load cage out," the captain said.

There was a burst of air beneath Alice's feet and the bottom of the ship shifted away and pistons popped above her.

"Cage locks disconnected. Dropping in five. Good luck out there."

Alice counted down in her head.

Three.

Two.

One.

The rails went loose and began to slide, giving Alice the familiar sensation of when a roller coaster starts to edge over the first dive.

Everything gave way and the entire drop cage went loose and hurdled through the air.

Her suit wasn't equipped to lock properly within the cage, but she squeezed the edges to keep from moving away.

American and European jets blasted by her, and on the ground a massive wave of creatures assaulted the military emplacements outside the city.

From this distance Berlin looked small, but the city was rapidly expanding before her eyes.

Dissension calibrators slid out on the side of the drop cage and came with small flaps that angled the cage at a desired spot. She looked over to see that Moller's cage was falling at the same rate.

There was a flash in the distance, and Alice saw the aircraft dropping bombs over thousands of tiny specs.

The horde.

There was a brighter flash as one of the aircraft spun out of control and careened into the ground. The cronux were bringing them down somehow.

That wasn't her fight though so she didn't focus on it.

Fuel jets beneath the cage kicked in and slowed her fall, but they were still coming in fast.

Alice steadied her breathing as she started to see the details on buildings and the things moving beneath.

Asphalt came up quickly and the cage slammed into it. Shock

absorbers steadied the cage, but Alice rattled around hard enough that she broke off the frontal lock and spilled out onto the ground.

This block had already been overrun and once-men charged at her the moment she came out. Alice didn't even have a chance to see how Moller landed.

The once-men grabbed at her CAG armor and lifted her off the ground. She reached for her rifle that was magnetically locked to her back, but something wrapped around her arm and pulled it tight.

A skinned woman came up against Alice's camera screens and blocked her view. The helmet flashed red warnings.

Alice struggled and they yanked her around and their fingers tried to find the grooves within her armor to pull the pieces apart.

There was no use in fighting, not in this world.

So Alice stepped into the other.

Alice left her body and entered into the void of the hive mind. A cold chill ran over her as she focused.

Her nude body stepped into the darkness and saw that it was thick with red lines.

She'd been here before. But she'd been tired and her mind stretched thin.

She was rested now, and her mind was focused.

With one hand she parted the red lines, and with the other, she grabbed a hold of a few, and pulled.

In the real world, Alice fell to the ground as the creatures all gave up their grip on her. Alice groaned as she got to her knees.

The once-men turned on each other. With a wild fury, they dug their fingers into one another and clawed out the parasites.

Alice stood up amongst the blood and screams of the melee and looked for Moller. She saw that Moller too had been dropped and was getting to her feet.

"You had me a little worried!" Moller shouted.

Alice gestured to her. "Let's go."

As a young man at war, Garin had worn a CAG and knew what it was like to fire his rifle at a man, but it had been decades since he was in the thick of it. Even in Leningrad, he was well away from the worst of the battle lines.

There were no lines here, and all of Berlin was a battlefield.

"Kill them!" Garin roared and pointed his rifle, fighting alongside a small team of loyal soldiers. The rifle bucked against his shoulder as it spat out bullet casings and pounded into the small goblinoid creatures.

They were ugly eyeless things with small heads and thick ears. One rushed at Garin from his cover behind a destroyed car. He pumped rounds into its chest until it collapsed dead mid-run, but others crawled over its dead body and jumped onto the car to spring on Garin and his team.

One jumped and Garin snatched it in mid air swung it to the ground with enough force from the CAG that it broke its spine while others lunged at his team, forcing them into close range combat.

There was a rumble a second before the dirt a few feet from Garin erupted, turning the car over on top of him. The worm burst into the open air and gave a hellish high pitch wail as it jerked about and spewed acid in all directions with abandon.

The acid hit buildings and ate through walls. It landed on the ground and burned up the asphalt. It hit a man in CAG and the man collapsed screaming as the armor melted away.

"Get this off me!" Garin screamed and his squad rushed over to get underneath the car. With a single mighty heavy, they lifted the car and Garin crawled out.

Someone helped lift him to his feet and he snatched his rifle from the ground. There was only a moment of pause before he had to aim and fire again at an oncoming creature.

The worm's mouth snapped closed and it sank down into the ground, leaving to go create havoc somewhere else.

Garin's team finished off the last of the goblinoids and opened his comms system with his other commanders to get status reports on the different lines of conflict, but a member of his team pointed into the sky.

"Sir, look!"

American and European warbirds screeched into view.

Garin gave them a nod, but there wasn't time for much else.

"*Status report,*" he barked into the comms.

ALICE WAS NOT ONE, but many. Her mind laced through the parasites.

She felt their hunger and their suffering, for their existence was that of misery.

And she saw all, for in this world, she had many eyes.

Blood was thrown upon her as the creatures savaged each other, tearing the parasites from each others' arms and shredding them apart.

Alice stood amongst the melee, her mind engaged in both worlds. She was the eye of the storm, the calm center of war.

An infected woman ripped the head off a man in front of her, as his spine disconnected, the blood splashed against her visor.

Alice didn't let it distract, she kept her head up. But her breathing was beginning to falter and she felt her chest tighten.

It was hard to remember to breathe with her focus spread so thin.

Her hand shook as she reached up and undid the clasps on her helmet. It popped and rose and she lifted it off, taking a breath of real air as her eyes rolled up into her head.

But she stayed on her feet in one world. . .

And pulled the red veins tight in the other.

Two dead boys battled one another and nearly careened into her, but Moller stepped in front and shoved them back into the crowd. They continued to struggle until they disappeared in the mass of legs and arms. The cronux tore at each other, but none reached for Alice, she only turned the hunger upon itself, and let it feast.

GARIN HAD TAKEN to a small building for a moment of calm to redirect the lines of combat. The outer perimeter was retreating, and there was a parasite outburst within a section of the city. Despite all the help the Western aircraft was offering, the bombing wouldn't win the battle.

Garin was reorganizing a movement to combat the infected section when he got a report over his comms.

"Sir, something is happening. There's a woman in the middle of them."

Garin pressed to respond, "If she's moving through them, she's already dead."

"No, sir, she's doing something to them. They're turning against each other."

Garin didn't understand. "Send me your video feed."

A second later a video feed played across Garin's screen.

The soldier sending the feed was on a rooftop looking down into a bloody melee. For whatever reason, the once-men had turned on each other, and in the center, a woman in American CAG stood with her hands held out while another woman moved around her, pushing away the creatures that fell in too close.

"Who the hell is that?" Garin asked.

"She's from an American dropship."

"Get the flame troopers down there. Clear her a path. I'm sending a pickup" Garin leaned up and stiffened his back. "Get her to me."

SOVIET SOLDIERS CAME up on the edges of the parasite mob and let loose a burst of flames.

Alice felt the strain of the hive mind ease as the parasites died. Her mind refocused and she picked up her helmet and fit it back on as the smell of burning bodies filled the air.

She took long breaths as she watched the creatures roll around in the fire, while the parasites shriveled and popped.

The flames were growing high, and a squad of Soviet soldiers stomped through them, the fire sizzling up alongside their armor.

"You are American?" a soldier said, his armor was scorched but he was unharmed. "Come with us."

Alice looked up into the air and saw swirling flocks of birds.

"Wait," she said.

Her mind reached up to the birds.

They were simple things. Their understanding and awareness was even less than the once-men.

It was an easy thing to cut their focus.

The little bodies rained down, smacking against buildings and smashing against the ground.

The swarm was dead.

"Let's go," Alice said.

———

THE JANISSARY WAS NOT PICKED for duty because of his strength or prowess.

It was because of his understanding of war.

He knew how to pick his moments.

This was not it.

He'd come prepared of course. He'd brought beings that moved with bellies full of acid and powerful brains that could calculate flight patterns and hurl themselves up into enemy aircraft.

But the bombers had gone higher, which was fine, he had expected as much. They simply needed a new method for the next encounter.

But he felt the birds die, their consciousness seemingly turned off.

Disconnected from him.

A curious thing indeed.

There'd also been a growing spread of parasites within the city, but that too had been stopped.

The Janissary knew by whom. . .

The woman.

. . .but how? That was another thing entirely.

This battle could not be won. He'd lost too many resources

already. Some could be easily spent, others were too valuable to be lost foolishly.

He was old in the ways of war.

He knew how to pick his moments.

Come.

He called Worm.

There would be another time for war.

The Janissary gathered his nearby brothers, and faded away into the forest.

ALICE LEFT with the Soviet soldiers and hurried through the streets. They were ambushed by a crowd of small goblinoids but Alice was able to shatter their minds and the soldiers blew them apart.

"We take you to Grand Marshal Garin," a soldier told her in accented English.

An armored personnel carrier arrived and she got in with Moller and one of the soldiers, while the others left to continue fighting.

But the battle was already over. Alice had felt him leave.

She felt the Janissaries warm, friendly touch against the grooves of her mind.

He slipped away but left her with a promise.

I will see you again.

The vehicle tore through the streets of Berlin with an urgency, but Alice breathed easy.

With the Janissary gone, the cronux would lose coordination.

They would be destroyed.

Berlin would live on.

Alice's comms were not patched to the Soviet's lines, nor did American communication stretch this far in. She could only speak with Moller, and they were both silent.

Sitting within the armored personnel carrier, with a moment of calm, it was only then that Alice became aware of the blood on her armor. She was coated red. It was so thick it leaked down her.

Alice sat in the back, her hands folded together and took deep breaths as she worked to pull her mind together, but it was hard. It felt like a hundred voices were screaming inside her.

It was as if every time her mind reached out. . .

The monsters inside her grew a little louder.

EPILOGUE

JOHN WINTERS SAT at his desk. He'd done nothing but stare at it for the last few hours.

"She might be the only one that can stop it."

That's what Roles had told him.

John didn't give a damn. The world asked too much of him, and now it wanted his daughter too.

How much must he give?

He agreed of course. What other choice did he have?

But he knew. . .

If she dies, John, it's your fault.

He'd been thinking that the whole time.

If she dies, it's your fault.

But she didn't die.

"She's still there now, she's safe," Roles confirmed. *"The Soviets are reporting that she met with Garin then spent the next few hours mopping up the creatures and dealing with outbreaks."*

Whatever relief John had when hearing she was safe quickly faded.

They're going to ask me to send her out again.

He knew that immediately.

The world would ask to put his daughter in the field again and again, and he had to wonder...

How many times can a person dodge death?

And how much can a man be asked to give?

WHILE MANY WERE CHEERING the good news of what Alice Winters did in Berlin, Roles was busy working.

Beijing popped.

That was what his contacts told him.

China was a country of one and a half billion people.

One and a half tightly packed, shoulder to shoulder, billion people.

And there was only one Alice Winters.

He would give John some time to settle and then Roles would work the man over. It was too torturous for John Winters to know what his daughter was doing. It would be better to take it out of his hands entirely.

Roles would oversee her.

As a person of special status, she'd have to be removed from the military chain of command all together.

She would be a Ghost.

But having just one Alice Winters might not be enough.

"I half expected them to shoot us," Moller told him over a secure comms link. *"It was a flip of the coin for them to think that maybe we were the ones that caused everything. Instead everyone saw her fighting in her blood soaked CAG, and now they cheer her. They're calling her the Red Bitch of Berlin. They love her."*

The Red Bitch of Berlin.

Roles liked that. The gamble had paid off.

"Moller," Roles said, "I have a new directive for you."

But no matter how good she was, one Alice Winters just wasn't enough.

"I need you to secure some live parasites."

WHAT'S NEXT?

Want to know the latest on the *Reality Bleed* series?

Join our Facebook group to talk *Reality Bleed* and keep up-to-date on everything that's happening.

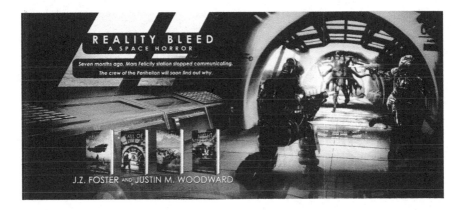

EARTH SIEGE

REALITY BLEED BOOK 8

ABOUT J.Z. FOSTER

J.Z. Foster is a writer originally from Ohio. He spent several years in South Korea where he met and married his wife.

He received the writing bug from his mother, NYTimes best-selling author, Lori Foster.

Check out his other books and let him know how you like them!

Write him an email at:
JZFoster@JZFoster.com

WINTER GATE PUBLISHING

Want to stay up to date on the latest from Winter Gate Publishing? Follow us on Facebook at Facebook.com/WinterGatePublishing to know more!

Winter Gate Publishing. Reality Bleed: Hold the Line

Made in the USA
Coppell, TX
02 June 2022

78407275R00115